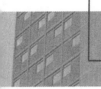

Tales of the
DeCongested

Volume One

Tales of the DeCongested, Volume One

Anthology of Short Stories read at Tales of the DeCongested

Edited by Paul Blaney and Rebekah Lattin-Rawstrone

Tales of the DeCongested, Volume One

Tales of the DeCongested is published by Apis Books, 5 Millennium Place, Bethnal Green, London E2 9NL.

ISBN 0-9552538-0-2

Editors:
Paul Blaney
Rebekah Lattin-Rawstrone

Apis Books would like to thank the Arts Council for making this project possible. We are grateful to the many people who have submitted and supported the event, the original sponsors of Tales of the DeCongested, Kitchen Garden Produce, and Foyles Bookshop for their continuing support.

For further copies or information, please contact Rebekah Lattin-Rawstrone, Apis Books, 5 Millennium Place, Bethnal Green, London E2 9NL. Tel: 07751 892825. Email: rebekah@apisbooks.com

Website: www.apisbooks.com

Typeset by Raffaele Teo

Printed and bound by Antony Rowe Ltd., Bumpers Farm, Chippenham, Wiltshire.

Table of Contents

Preface

Tales of the DeCongested was conceived in October 2003, on a SouthWest train stalled between Vauxhall and Waterloo. Returning from a profitable evening at the Wimbledon greyhounds, and temporarily unable to continue our journey, we fell to lamenting the status of the short story in Britain. By the time our train limped to its destination, we'd resolved to take up arms. Short story writers can seldom publish their work but why should that stop them performing it? Clearly what was needed was a live short story-reading event.

In the course of the next weeks, we booked a venue, sent out calls in all directions for submissions, and, of course, got ourselves a website (www.decongested.com). Our first venue, intimate and informal, was the Poetry Café in Covent Garden. Stories poured in; authors were invited to read; we set out the chairs, but would there be an audience? It felt – and has continued to feel – like throwing a once-a-month party and wondering, as we arranged the Pringles and mixed the punch, would anyone come?

Fortunately, our instinct had not misled us. People came that first night and have continued to come in increasing numbers. Odd as this might appear to some, there are many Londoners who, at the end of a working week, can think of nothing better to do with their Friday night than sit and listen to urgent, suspenseful and beautifully written stories – just so long as they get to the pub by nine o'clock. After that first year, we took the decision to move to a larger, purpose-built venue on the second floor of Foyles bookshop, Charing Cross Road.

Tales developed and we discovered fresh talent as strange, surprising stories materialised in our Inbox. Following the last-Friday-of-the-month events, many of these stories appeared on our website. At the same time, in order to reach a wider audience, we planned to produce a selection of the finest tales in book form. We had an embarrassment of talent to choose from, but publishing that talent was easier said than done.

Ask any agent or publisher, and they'll tell you there's no market for short stories in Britain. Certainly, the short story is a different beast from the novel, more condensed and requiring closer attention. Short stories (such as those contained here), however, generously reward that attention, a fact of which their readers are well aware. To argue that there is no market for them in Britain is short-sighted – as if there were something peculiar about 'the British reader' that made him or her immune to the short story. Where excellent work is properly promoted there will always be a market.

In January of 2006 we received Arts Council funding and our desire to publish an anthology became a possibility. When Ali Smith and Nicholas Royle, both of whom have read at Tales, offered to contribute a short story apiece, it began to seem more than just possible. And so we, along with Justine Shaw and Dom Nemer, founded a company, Apis Books (www.apisbooks.com), in order to produce this volume and, we hope, others that will raise the profile of shorter fiction. We then spent several weeks selecting and arguing over our favourite stories in order to arrive at the final thirty-five.

We could wax lyrical about the virtues of these stories, but we'd rather you just went ahead and sampled them for yourselves. In line with the times and also with the performance roots of Tales of the DeCongested, you can do so either by reading them on the printed page or by going to www.apisbooks.com where live recordings of the stories will be available for download in due course. Most of the authors chose to read their own stories, bringing to the recording some of the flavour of the live event.

Thanks are in order. First of all, we'd like to thank the Arts Council, and secondly our original landlord, The Poetry Café, and more recent hosts, Foyles. Further thanks to our loyal audience and to anyone who's ever had the considerable guts to submit a story to Tales – and face the even more dreadful prospect of being asked to perform it. Most of all, thanks are due to the authors whose stories appear in this volume. We sincerely wish we could offer payment in more than contributor's copies – writing stories is hard work and worthy of recompense – and hope to do so in the case of future volumes. We certainly don't mean this to be the last you'll hear of Tales of the DeCongested.

As co-editors of a short story collection, we ought to appreciate that brevity is a virtue. We'd best not ramble, get long-winded, expatiate, or take you round the houses. One last thing though – the name. Let's just say that Tales of the DeCongested mixes Roald Dahl with a dash of Mayor Ken to produce fiction that will neither block our streets nor destroy our air quality. Some of the stories in the pages ahead may, however, make you laugh; they may make you think, smile, weep, purr, kiss your boss, or even miss your stop. They might even tempt you along to Foyles one of these last-Fridays to take in some live action. Or could they persuade you to take up your pen (click on your keyboard) and write something yourself? Who knows where this might end? Let the reader beware!

Rebekah Lattin-Rawstrone & Paul Blaney

Ali Smith

The Present

There were only three people in The Inn: a man at the bar, the barmaid, and me. The man was chatting up the barmaid. The barmaid was polishing glasses. I was waiting for a pub supper I'd ordered half an hour ago. I was allowing myself one double whisky. It was a present to myself.

Have you seen them, covered in all the frost? the man was saying to the barmaid. Don't they look just like magic roofs, don't they look like winter always looked when you were a little child?

The barmaid ignored him. She held the glass up to the light to see if it was clean. She polished it some more. She held it up again.

The man gestured towards the pub's front window.

Go out and look at it. Just have a look at it, look at it on the roofs, the man said. Don't they look exactly like what winter was like when you were small? Like white came over everything by magic, like a giant magician waved his hand and a white frost came down over everything.

You don't half talk a load of wank, the woman behind the bar said.

Her saying this made me laugh so suddenly that I choked on the drink I was taking. They both looked round. I coughed, turned away slightly towards the fire, and went on looking at my paper like I was reading it.

I heard them shift their attention back towards each other.

It's Paula, isn't it? he said.

She said nothing.

It's definitely Paula, he said. I remember. I asked you before. Remember? I was here, I was in this very pub about six weeks ago. Remember?

She held another glass up and looked at it.

Well, I remember you, he said.

She put it down and picked up another. She held it up between her and the light.

So if you don't like Christmas and so on, Paula, he said. If you don't think it's a magic time from our childhoods and so on. Well, why'd you bother to decorate the pub, then? Why'd you bother to spray the snowy stuff on the door and the windows. Why'd you make the place look like snow off Christmas cards? It's only November, after all. It's not even December.

It's not my pub, the woman said. I don't get to choose when Christmas begins and ends.

The whisky I'd choked on had gone down the wrong way and had formed a burning gutter along the inside of my windpipe. I ignored it. I read my paper. It was about how the Gulf Stream was being eroded at an almighty rate. Soon it would be as cold as Canada here in the winter. Soon the snow outside would be six feet high every winter and winter would last from October till April.

Magic roofs, the woman said. Christ. See the house with the Alfa Romeo outside it?

The man went to the door and opened it.

I can't see an Alfa Romeo from here, he said.

The third-along car from the left, she said without raising her voice.

I saw some cars, but I'll take your word for it that one's an Alfa, he said coming back in.

They call him the German in the village, she said. His name's German-sounding. He never comes in here. He hit black ice round the Ranger Bend with his two sons in the car two years ago and the son that was in the front seat died. The car hasn't moved from outside that house since it came back from the garage with a new side on it. He walks to work, he walks out his gate and past it every day. We all go past it every day. He had a German-sounding name and all, the son, I mean. He was eleven or twelve. He never came in here before it, the father I mean, the German, and he never comes in now. And the house next to his. That's where the girl lives who's in debt because of the pyramid.

Egypt? the man said.

Scheme, the women said. Not to tell tales or nothing, but I was at Asda and I heard her telling someone on her mobile that she had a dream.

The man leaned on the bar.

You're a dream, Paula, he said.

This is her dream, the woman said. Would you believe it? An angora jumper she'd bought on her credit card had, listen to this, upped and left home because it was unhappy living with her. Then the jumper phoned her from the airport but because it couldn't speak, because jumpers can't, can they, she didn't know what it was trying to say.

An angry jumper? the man said.

No, an angora jumper, the woman said. It's a kind of wool, a warm expensive kind. And the house next to that. His daughter's a druggie. Whenever she comes back to the village he won't let her in the front door. First she throws stones at the living room window. Then the old bloke calls the police. The house next to that. Divorced. He had an affair. She got custody. He's a nice guy. He works in the city. She's a teacher. She's got a Cinquecento.

She held up a glass, examined it against the light.

The house next to them, she said.

Uh huh? he said.

That's my house, she said.

You're not married are you, Paula? the man said.

You are, the woman said. I can tell a mile off.

I'm not married, the man said. I'm single as the day is long.

This time of year you'll be less single, then, she said.

You what? he said.

The days being shorter and all, the woman said.

What you laughing at? the man said. What you looking at?

He was talking to me. I pretended I hadn't heard or understood.

What's she think she's looking at? the man said.

Won't be long, the woman called over to me. Sorry to keep you waiting.

No worries, I said. It's fine.

She went through the door at the back. Have you not thawed out the scampi? she was shouting as she went.

The man stared at me. There was quite a lot of hostility in his stare. I could feel it without me even looking back properly. When the woman came through from the kitchen and put down in front of me, like a firm promise that I would definitely be fed, condiments, and a knife and fork both neatly wrapped in a napkin, he shouted over at me from his place at the bar.

You agree with me. Don't you? You think it looks like magic, he said. Like a magician off a TV programme when we were kids just, you know, waved his hand in the sky over all our home towns and down came the whiteness.

He started to come over; he looked like he might actually punch me if I said I disagreed. But when he reached the table I could see he was less drunk than he seemed. It was almost as if he was pretending to be more drunk than he was. He sat down on the stool across the table from me. He wasn't much older than me. His face was crumpled, like a piece of wrapping that someone had tried to squeeze in a fist into as small as possible a ball.

I looked down at my knife and fork wrapped in the napkin. There were little cartoon sprigs of holly all over the napkin.

The man picked the HP sauce bottle up out of the arrangement of salt and pepper and mustard and vinegar sachets and sauce bottles in front of me.

You know what the H and the P stand for on a bottle of HP? he said.

Houses of Parliament, I said.

His face fell. He looked truly disappointed that I knew. I pointed to the picture on the bottle's label. I shrugged.

You're not from round here, he said. Didn't think so, he said. Something about your shape of face. Don't get me wrong, he said. It's a nice shape of face. I'm from fifty miles from here, he said. Originally, I mean. What you drinking, then? he said.

He said it all very loudly, as if he was saying it not really to me but for the barmaid back behind the bar to hear.

How about I tell you, he said, putting his foot up on the low stool nearest me, about what Christmas means to me? Shall I tell you two girls what a really happy Christmas is?

I looked at his foot in its scuffed shoe on the plush of the bar stool. I could see the colour of his socks. They were light brown. Someone had bought him those socks as a present maybe, or maybe someone had bought them because he was lucky enough to have someone routinely care about his socks. Or, if not, he had gone into a shop and bought them himself. But this was the last thing I wanted to care about, a detail like where someone else's socks had come from. I had been out driving around since about half past four this morning. I had driven into the car park of this pub tonight precisely because I believed there would be nobody here I knew, nobody here who would bother me, nobody here who would ask anything of me, nobody here who would want to speak to me about anything, anything at all.

I looked at the man's foot again with the thin line of human skin there between the top of the sock and where the edge of his trouser leg began. I stood up. I got my car keys out of my pocket.

Going somewhere? the man said.

The barmaid was taking packets of peanuts off little hooks above the till, dusting them and putting them back. She turned as I went past.

Won't be much longer, five minutes at the most, she called after me.

I pushed the door open regardless and went out of The Inn.

But I was two new whiskies down, I realised as I slid into the driver's seat. I couldn't drive anywhere, not for a good while. I sat in the car in the lit car park and watched the sign that said The Inn hang motionless beyond the windscreen, which had immediately steamed up with the warmth coming off me. There was no wind tonight. That was why it was so frosty. It was cold out, bitterly cold. It would soon be bleak midwinter.

I put the key in the ignition and pushed the button which turns the seat-heating on. Cars were great. They were full of things that simply, mechanically, met people's needs. Inside seat-heating. Adjustable seat levers. Little vanity mirrors in the windscreen shades. Roof that slides right back if you want it to.

I began to try to guess what story the man would have told two virtual strangers in a pub to prove what made a good Christmas. The best Christmas lunch he'd ever eaten. The best present anyone ever gave him. It would be something about his childhood since that was all he'd really wanted to talk about in there, childhood and lost magic, and the coming back of magic at the coldest of times in the back of beyond in the form of a simple frost that catches the light in the dark.

Imagine if we had all been friends in that bar, had been people who really had something to say, had wanted to talk to each other.

Now you, I imagined the barmaid saying to me, perched on one of those too-high stools above me and him, so that leaning down and forking up one of my scampi pieces for herself was a little precarious, but she wavers perfectly, balances perfectly, tucks the scampi into her mouth and we all laugh together at her expertise, including herself.

Your turn, she says. A really happy one, come on.

Well, okay, though happy's not the word I'd have used at the time, I say. I'm about twelve.

I don't mean this to sound rude, but you look a bit older than twelve, the man says.

Not now. Obviously. In the story, I say.

Okay, the man says.

Okay, the barmaid says.

And in my neighbourhood there's this new couple that's moved in a couple of streets down, and everybody knows them, everyone knows who they are I mean, because they're a husband and wife teaching couple, they both teach modern languages at the school all the local kids go to, the school I go to.

Not very Christmassy so far, the barmaid says.

Give her a chance, the man says. She'll get to it. Some time in the near future.

Christmas Past, Christmas Present, Christmas Near-Future, the barmaid (Paula) says.

Anyway, the Fenimores, Mr and Mrs Fenimore, I say. Mr Fenimore is really pioneering. He's small and slim, but always looks like he's setting out on an adventure with an imaginary hiking stick in his hand.

I know the type, Paula says.

He takes over the after-school chess and judo clubs, I say. He starts up an after-school cookery class and he takes a lot of flak for being a man who runs a cookery class. Mrs Fenimore helps. She always helps. She is always there helping, she's a shy person who smiles a lot, while her husband, whom she looks at with eyes full of a sad, hopeful love, runs the school clubs, and not just those, he forms a neighbourhood wine club where our parents and the other neighbours who don't have kids go to the Fenimores' house to taste wine, Mrs Fenimore puts invitations through everybody's door, smiling shyly if you look out the window and see her on her rounds. JACK AND SHIRLEY FENIMORE INVITE YOU TO A SPECIAL WINE TASTING. Loads of people go, all the neighbours go, my mother and father go, and they never usually go to anything. They've never done anything like it before. Then everybody talks about how nice the Fenimores are, how much they like the Fenimores' house, car, garden, cutlery, design of plates. Then the Fenimores organise a theatre visit. JACK AND SHIRLEY FENIMORE INVITE YOU TO EDUCATING RITA AT

THE EMPIRE. Everybody goes. JACK AND SHIRLEY FENIMORE INVITE YOU TO A MULLED WINE EXTRAVAGANZA. JACK AND SHIRLEY FENIMORE INVITE YOU ON A SOLSTICE ASSAULT ON BEN WYVIS.

Assault on Ben who? the man (I'll call him Tom) says.

No, I say. Ben Wyvis is a mountain. Ben is a Scottish word for mountain.

Yeah, I know, I know that, Tom says.

You don't know nothing, Paula says. You didn't know what angora was a minute ago.

Anyway, I say. About twenty of us, who've all lived under Ben Wyvis for most of our lives and have never been up it, about seven adults and the rest kids my age, some younger, a couple of older ones, get into a minibus the Fenimores hire, because Mr Fenimore's just got his minibus driving licence, and drive to the foot of Ben Wyvis to see how high up it we can get on the Sunday before Christmas, December 21st, a gloriously sunny Sunday, bright and crisp and blue-skied. And then what happens?

You get to the top and you have the most fantastic party, Tom says, and you kiss your first boy up a romantic mountain on the shortest day of the year.

The minibus breaks down, Paula says. You never even leave the neighbourhood.

Halfway up the mountain, I say, the sky changes colour from blue to black, and half an hour later it starts to snow. It snows so heavily that seven adults and twelve or thirteen kids get snowed into a space under a crag on Ben Wyvis. It's before the days of mobile phones. There's no way of letting anyone know where we are. It's freezing. We huddle together; then the adults huddle the kids inside a circle of their bodies. It gets dark. It doesn't stop snowing. All there is is snow in the dark, and more snow, and dark at the back of it, snow for miles of empty sky, and a lot of swearing from my father, he's dead now, and the man from across the road, he's dead now too I think, threatening to murder Mr Fenimore, and my mother who'd worn shoes with heels on to go up a mountain in, my mother, she'd never even been on a hike before never mind anywhere near a mountain, cursing herself, and a bit of arguing about who should go for help, and Mrs Fenimore crying, and Mr Fenimore counting heads every five minutes, before he sets off into the white dark to bring help back.

Oh god, Tom says. Does he die?

It ends happily, Paula says. Doesn't it?

Mr Fenimore is lost on the hill till the next day, when the rescue services pick him up, I say. He's in hospital for a week. We're all already home by then. We all get picked up about an hour later by three men in a helicopter. The father of a girl called Jenny McKenzie, in the year above me at school, has phoned the rescue services and told them where we went, after he picked up the bad forecast on the radio. They keep four of us in hospital overnight, including me. It's a laugh. We're all fine. But the thing is, we get home and – there's no snow anywhere. None. It's all just like normal, like none of it happened.

Then what? Tom says.

What happened about the Fenimores? Paula says.

How was that a happy Christmas? Tom says.

I had no idea what happened to the Fenimores, I realised, sitting there by myself in my warmed-up seat in my car in a near-empty car park, miles from home. I could remember her sad face. I could remember his open, naïve brow, his forward slant when he walked down the school corridor, or up the makings of a path at the foot of the ben. They were only there for that year, maybe. They moved away. The judo club stopped. A home economics teacher took over cookery club. People stopped talking about them like they were the local joke pretty soon. Where were those people, the hopeful man and his sad, helpful love, where were the Fenimores tonight, nearly thirty years later? Were they warm in a house, well into their middle-age? Were they still the Fenimores?

From here in my car I could see the frosty roofs on the village terrace below, down at the bottom of the slope. I looked the other way and saw, through the side window of the pub, the man and the barmaid.

The man had his back to the bar. He was holding a near-empty glass, staring ahead into space. The barmaid was leaning on her elbow. She was staring in the opposite direction. They stayed like that, unmoving, like figures in a painting, the whole time I watched.

The barmaid was called Paula. I had no idea what the man's name was. Good, because I didn't want to know. I was just a stranger who ordered supper and didn't eat it. I was long gone, as far as they knew, on the road out of here in the dark.

I put my hand on the ignition key, whisky or no whisky.

But if I went back inside, I could eat. And if I went back inside, if I was simply there, those two people would speak to each other again, they'd be able to, even if I was just sitting reading my paper or eating my supper ignoring them.

I looked down at the roofs of the houses sheened with the fierce frost, like a row of far away houses in the kind of story we tell ourselves about winter and its chancy gifts.

I opened the car door and got out. I locked it, though I probably didn't need to, and I went back into the pub.

Tadeusz Deręgowski

The Bloody Sock and Other Tales

I had decided to commit suicide. I had decided that some times before, but always something had come in my way: a telephone call, the chance encounter with a friend. It was so hard to find the peace to do anything.

This time, I had decided to gas myself in my car. I had seen an actor do it on television; it didn't look that hard. I remember the day well: balmy. A speckle of rain touched the windscreen as I sat in the car, ready to drive off.

Then I was on the highway; then I was at the filling station. I felt hungry so I bought myself a Star Bar. Normally these give me flatulence so I don't eat them, but I figured that I wouldn't be around to suffer. Let the coroner be the one to hold his nose!

I found a B-road off the highway. The road was quiet and I relaxed, so I stopped there in the driveway to a field. A few elders and beech trees clustered there. I got a hose from the boot and drew it through the back window from the exhaust. Then I sat back in the driver's seat. I unwrapped the Star Bar and began to munch it, thinking of nothing in particular, just enjoying the crisp cereal and milk chocolate mixture churning in my gob. I wanted that pleasure before turning the ignition.

But, as my luck would have it, another car drove up to a halt behind mine: a red Ford Fiesta. In it was an elderly couple. I could see them in my mirror begin to eat sandwiches from a plastic box. How long would they be? They seemed to chew very slowly. I calculated perhaps ten minutes. Boredom.

Then I saw the man nod towards my car and the woman adjust her glasses to see better. Oh no! They had spotted the hose. With doddering steps the man came towards my car. He rapped on the side window. I felt myself turn crimson with embarrassment.

I tried to ignore him, gazing straight ahead intently, but I could sense his face peering through the glass at my profile and hear his rapping again. His wife came up too. I could hear her voice.

"Is he all right? Open the door. See if he's all right."

The man opened the door. What a fool I was! I should have locked it.

"Are you all right?" said the man.

"Oh yes. Yes, I'm fine," I said.

"There's a hose going from the exhaust into your car," said the man.

"That's dangerous," said the woman.

"You could kill yourself like that," said the man.

I stared ahead, trying to ignore them. Then I felt a sudden burst of flatulence from the Star Bar. I could not, to my embarrassment, contain it, and with a fearsome raspberry had to relieve myself. The car filled with a repulsive gust of Cadbury's.

With my flatulent outburst, the couple concluded that I was beyond reason. They called the police – I must say, I resented that: after all, I was harming no-one other than myself – and I spent the better part of the following six months discussing the human condition with a gentle Pakistani doctor and an earnest PhD student. I liked the doctor and I liked the student, and I sincerely hope that the stories I told him about my childhood experiences of bestiality helped him write an amusing thesis.

A few months later I found myself with a little money in my pocket and an abnormally cheerful mood, the day full of sunshine, standing on the rise of Upper Street looking down to London, wondering quite what to do.

Then it occurred to me. I should buy myself a parrot. If I had a parrot, then I would not want for company. Why, the bird would be kept in a cage, it could not escape me even if it wished to. And it would be sure to talk nothing but sense, for I would teach it aphorisms by La Rochefoucauld and it might even learn one or two of my own sage pronouncements!

At the pet shop, I asked the girl for a parrot.

"There is this one," she said.

"I see," I said. The parrot was huge, its iridescent plumage dazzling: a true aristocrat of the parrot world. "How much is it?" I asked.

"It is seven hundred pounds."

"That seems dear," I said.

"He speaks French as well as English," she replied.

"I see," I said.

The conversation went on like that, quite conventionally, but I found myself falling into a daze, and I wandered out of the shop without the parrot. I am like that; I just get bored and leave situations.

The day had turned sallow. Thoughts began to trouble my mind: that the world was inside out. You might encounter a couple who had for years wished to have children, then had given birth to a handicapped child. You might have thought to pity that child with its slow mind and clumsy gait, facing exclusion from childhood games which so often required rapid co-ordination. Or, in the trials of adolescence, how the sexual favours that came with grace and beauty would be denied her, and copulation would remain a weird, purely theoretical possibility. But that girl might then develop a skill to compensate for her handicaps, becoming a fine player of winsome melodies on a golden harp, or cultivating yellow roses, investing patience and love in study, nurturing talents to glorify herself and the experience of others.

Then you, yourself, might become the victim of a misfortune, or a depression, or your own pusillanimity, and that selfsame girl whom you had pitied and, in her youth, regarded so woefully, now comes to offer her music to give you consolation, or her yellow roses to bring you cheer.

Oh yes, indeed, the world was full of strange events like that. There was nothing that was not open to equivocation.

Why, I had even encountered a couple living in my block. They had arrived home to find a sock, bloody, in the middle of the living room floor. What purpose was there in that discovery? And inside the sock, five severed digits! It quite consternated them; they talked about it for days after. They even mentioned it to their neighbours. And the cleaning that had to be done to remove the blood from the Persian carpet; it was so unfair! All that trouble because of a bloody sock!

I met them on the stairs. They stood close together; the trauma had served to unite them in horror. They stood there in a dim silence, their earlier loquaciousness overtaken by a sullen mood, resenting a world that could so dishonour their living room floor. I asked them if they had reported the incident to the concierge but they did not, I think, want to talk about it. "Ah well," I sighed, in what I hoped was a sympathetic manner.

In truth, however, I felt ill at ease with my neighbours from then on, and I am sure that the atmosphere that prevailed in our block became odd, taut, uneasy; a callow silence in the stairwell, as if we were all guilty, but unsure quite of what. The ladies who lived on the first floor were forever gossiping in mumbles over their mops and brooms and watching from their landing the, now notorious, front door.

And after an event like that your life might end. You might simply explode at a street corner while waiting for the green man, or expire quietly in the middle of a dream about geraniums and chocolate éclairs or a childhood game such as hopscotch. There were some who took their lives in despair; that seemed romantic but normally the lives of the suicides were merely bedevilled by petty wickednesses: debts, chronic illnesses, the abuse of schoolchildren, the malign effects of drugs. Truly, there was no glamour to their wretchedness.

I awoke from my thoughts to birdsong and a rustling of leaves. An angel with a broken cross gazed plaintively; from some evergreens a cherub peeped.

I had wandered into a cemetery. I was seated on a bench.

What about the parrot? I went back and got it.

Tadeusz Derȩgowski

The Drive Home

I had wished to write a story to do with my workplace, V.E.M. Engineering (components manufacturers for domestic appliances), but when I began to write the subject receded from me and I was left with nothing after even an hour of trying.

And so, I shall press on with other matters, or should I say, let other matters press on to me, for I cannot say that I have chosen this that I am, nor the things that move me.

As I was driving home I remembered that I had to stop off at the supermarket, because I had arranged to go to Peggy's for supper, and I felt it incumbent upon me to bring something. Peggy cooked well, and her larder was well stocked and her fridge too – she liked shopping and had a developed interest in food. The food itself was not the problem.

The problem I was about to solve by going to the supermarket was this: that I felt guilty about our relationship. I felt guilty because I knew I could never love her and I knew that she deserved love. I also knew that she had not been loved in her life because her heart was too open, so that she gave too soon and too easily and was taken for granted.

I pitied her for that, and with my pity came a sense of shame, and to compensate for my shame I thought of bringing her some cheese to go with the meal, as if she would not notice that I did not love her if I brought her something as one who truly loved her would have done.

I smiled as I drove and thought of the cheese. I remembered my father then; his image faded into my mind's eye as I drove. He was there at the dining table, large and proselytising about Italian cheese. The British had been duped, he pronounced. They had been deceived into believing that French cheese was superior to Italian cheese. But, he remonstrated loudly, they were wrong. What was French cheese but an endless variation on Brie, with peppercorns or fruit foolishly thrown in for the sake of novelty? And Roquefort compared to Gorgonzola? And could any French cheese possibly rival that very King of Cheeses, Parmesan?

He was from Piedmont and I suspect that the issue was partly a matter of patriotism for him.

As I thought of that I felt the need to weep, so I pulled over to the hard shoulder and wept on that evening drive home, for my father had died the week before.

When I arrived at Peggy's she asked me if the traffic was bad, because I was seldom late. I said that it was and did not mention the weeping.

Eyes closed, Robert lies in bed listening to Cynthia clattering around the house. The sneezings, coughings, slappings, rufflings, knockings and bangings have become a strangely reassuring prelude to his day. They yo-yo him in and out of consciousness, until he, too, is fully awake.

He imagines her fingers sliding through her thick, damp hair, temples being massaged by long, slender thumbs. Her head hurts – it must. Hurt like her brains are going to explode and she struggles to keep them in. They're becoming a regular feature, the Sunday afternoon drinking sessions. It's a worry, but he says nothing. And he had to manhandle her home last night, back here to this very bed upon which he undressed her.

And though he knew he shouldn't, he did.

The hish of slippers on floorboards: she makes her way back into the bedroom. Though he is by far the heavier of the two, his are the tiny toe-scurries of a ballerina compared to her baby elephant steps. Hers a farmyard childhood with acres of rooms to charge around in; his full of whispers in suburban box rooms, father in the study working, always working. Eggshells and tiptoes, he learned to walk like a princess.

Slurps: she tilts a mug of coffee to and from her lamb-chop-pink lips.

The click-click of the lighter as she fires up a Benson.

Sometimes she looks up into his face with such gravity and says, Do you love me? Of course, he says. Then she says, But I love you more. Yes, but my love for you is wider, he says, stretching out his arms and fingertips. She does the same, and they are crucified lovers, his chin resting on the top of her head.

That's so unfair, she faux-whines into his chest. Arms fold into an embrace, he envelops her and whispers, I could not love you more, silly.

Eight months may be a short time, but already their love is the colour of years.

He imagines her dressing gown wrapped around her skin, and he wonders, Does she remember?

The question rattles inside his skull.

That is the drawer being slid open: the knickers and bra drawer. That is the brisk swish of fabric against skin: she pulls her knickers on. Then with her back to him – lest he rolls over and sees – she pushes the dressing gown from her shoulders, lets it fall to the floor: a gentle fudumph noise. She sucks air through her teeth and removes yesterday's white sports bra, replacing it with a similar one. She pulls it over her head, arms through the thick straps.

And then she slips it into the left side.

They always make love in the dark. She floats high above him, hips lushing like waves against the shore, the band of her bra like a beacon moving closer, closer still, then a pale shadow soaring away from him. She makes soft sounds as he watches, and sometimes he gets lost in the theatre of it all and reaches up to touch her. But she pins him down, fire-eyes glowering in the bedroom dark.

The wardrobe door creaks, hangers rattle. She's putting her uniform on. Its colour: the blue of Milk of Magnesium. That tight blue uniform she wears in the salon where she works on the high street. He inadvertently ripped the last one in a moment of not uncommon spontaneity. But a spontaneity that always has to be controlled.

He didn't plan to do it. He wasn't thinking. But she opened her eyes for a brief moment, blinking up into his face, and she must have seen the expression written there, for the apostrophe of a solitary tear, lit in the lamplight, slithered down her cheek. She rolled away from him, pulling the sheet over the exposed skin. He wanted to hold her then, to tell her over and over again that he was sorry, that what he had just done was unforgivable, but surely it didn't matter because they loved each other more than...

But he couldn't.

He dashed out into the garden and clung to the fence, breathing deep, just breathing. The sound of the beck at the bottom of the garden coming to him – an airy dialogue passed between them.

She is dragging the brush through her hair. Swishing, tearing sounds, removing knots – she calls them cotters. She takes great pride in her hair now; she never thought it would be this long again. Now it's as long as his, the same colour too – a demerara beige, she calls it. They are often mistaken for brother and sister, except that his eyes are a periwinkle, almost Listerine green, and hers a burnt umber, Malteser brown.

The bed moves as she sits down.

He wishes she would snuggle herself around his warm body, bury her face into his hair. With this thought, he lets a thin smile buckle his lips, then he fights to unbend it because she might remember, and what would she think to a smile like this?

Of course he makes mistakes.

Drunk, he often lies in bed next to her, stroking her face, arms, her legs, begging her to let him at her 'good' breast. Sorry, she always says. I just can't. She'll chart a line of pitter-patter kisses down onto his hunger, turning it in on him. Fold it, overlap it, till he is released and soft with love.

Once he tried to get in the shower with her. She curled herself up in the corner and screamed blood to her face: GET OUT YOU ABSOLUTE FUCKING BASTARD. Days passed before she would let him hold her again, breathlessly pounding his chest.

Bastard. Bastard. Bastard.

She exhales through her teeth, then the cigarette to her lips: a few pt-pt sounds as she takes it down to the butt. I thought you would have given up, he remembers saying. She laughed out smoke and said, What's the point?

He pictures her taking a drowsy look at the pile of clothes concertina'd across the floor, shed taxingly only a few hours ago, perhaps trying to recall how she got home.

Pt... pt-pt... pt...

But last night he looked.

He was alarmed by the size of it. The crude butchery stretching from the top of her armpit to her sternum. Inches of it. Inches with a brown splodge of nipple at the centre. Twisted, flat, misshapen. He was surprised that she even had a nipple, expecting just the whole thing to be gone. It was so unlike how he'd imagined. It was meant to be small and neat, not that Frankenstein disfigurement, not that crude slasher's seam, as if the surgeon had used a rusty spoon to cut through the skin and scoop out her lymph and breast tissue. Yes, it would be neat and thin, and he would trace its delicate line with his tongue. And with the fever of youth, that animal bed-soaking lust in their veins, they would submerge, diving into one another. In the morning he would shove her silicone falsie down his pants and parade around the bedroom like a Chippendale. Christ, how she would laugh, gasping for breath. Once shame-withered and cautious, now blossoming into careless pride.

I'm in remission.

Her expression refused to echo the pure hopefulness of the statement. She has to go to the hospital every three months. If only the specialist's certitude meant something to her.

But I know I haven't got long. It's just around the corner. You are my last chance at Love.

He wears the hat of the listener then, the hat of the patient carer. But the hat is fake and simply does not fit nor suit him. He rummages through his imaginary hatbox for one more honest, but after a while his feet lead him from that room to another, to be alone with his unutterable, disloyal fears.

Sometimes when he holds her he wishes his good cells could enter hers, cleanse her in some way.

Sometimes when he is inside her he feels that he is fucking the grave.

Shuffling noises along to the head of the bed-is she leaning over, looking? She pulls the thin sheet back a little, over his shoulder. Then a little more, until it's past his thigh. She brushes a few strands of hair from his cheek. He pictures his body: soft and rounded against hers: lithe, pale, almost muscular.

He feigns the symptoms of being woken. He catches his breath, fearing the words, wishing he could rewind the film of the previous night, alter it somehow, chop it up, splice it out, cut the entire scene.

Hello.

He will have to open his eyes for he can't escape it.

She quizzes him softly, And how come you're so awake this morning?

He flashes his eyes up at her, blinkingly, through sleep-jumbled hair. He is shocked; in the darkness of the room he can just make it out: she is wearing make-up; mascara, a touch of dark eyeshadow, and lipstick – Pepto-Bismol pink.

He pulls her warm body down onto him and kisses her neck, the heady, familiar scent of the woman he adores gently strumming the strings of his libido.

She speaks into his neck, Jesus. Was I totally off it last night?

Waves. Waves of anxiety flush over him.

Yeah, something like that.

He holds her at arm's length, and his gaze wanders from the strangeness of her made-up face to the left bulge in her dress, and he thinks she sees him looking. He rolls over, pulling the bedsheet back up to his chin.

What he takes as love is already beginning to disappear inside of itself, folding up, cut like paper, an origami duck, something awkward with sharp edges that move if you touch them. The duck opens its wings and flaps about inside him. He asks it to leave, he tells himself that he is just being silly, but his body is a cage of fear and disgust.

He steals a quick glance at the smiling clock: twenty-past-eight. Six hours and he'll be back in that too-big, quiet office at the factory, waiting for him and his worries to fill the sweet-scented air, the silence punctuated by the secretary's machine gun rat-a-tat-tatting on the plastic QWERTY.

He feels it: she's watching the back of his head, thinking her secret thoughts. The bed sinks behind him again as she moves. The softness of her lips and warmth of her breath dance upon his cheek. A sweet Love You floats into his ear before she moves off the bed, picks up her jacket, and jingles the keys off the hook.

He sighs then inhales, about to shout I LOVE YOU back.

But it's too late; she's gone.

He lies in the bedroom dark, and his thoughts retreat to the night they first met, the residue of that night still unwithered in his mind. I'm Rob, the man called Robert had said. And I'm Cynth, the woman called Cynthia had said. Then she said, You're pretty short, and he said something like, Yeah well, I'm afraid of heights. And it went on like this, revealing themselves in giddy, babbled increments. And there were no awkward, petulant silences then. No aloof mimes or silly gestures. Just witticisms and peals of laughter. Peals of light-hearted, carefree, impossible-to-stop laughter.

He opens the bedroom curtains. Grey morning light fills the room like a headache. He pulls the bedside cabinet drawer open and removes a small, leather-bound Filofax. One of the inside pockets holds a photograph, secreted from Cynthia's album. He climbs back into bed and carefully slides the photograph out.

A picture of Cynthia, lying on a beach somewhere, her skin the colour of butternut squash turning to tan. Aubergine-purple bikini bottoms, skimpy, wet-looking as if she'd just walked out of the sea. One leg raised, lazily. He doesn't know who took the photograph – he just hopes it wasn't a man.

Look at them: two breasts – two perfect, faultless breasts. And the skin from her underarm to her breastbone – baby-soft. Flawless.

He wonders if the cancer was already doing its wrong.

He thinks of other men, taking, touching, kissing, sucking. Or worse still – ignoring.

He so desperately wants the origami duck to become a swan, a dazzling white swan, and for the swan to appear before her every time they make love now, for her not only to see the swan mirrored there but to feel that the reflection belongs to her as she floats high above, hips breaking like waves against him. He wants her pale shadow to be cast into the deep waters so that he can hold it there forever, in case – as she keeps insisting – she ever goes. In case this thing disappears completely.

He wants his soul to be the mirror of her looking, and of her laughing.

He jumps out of bed, and trying to walk with baby elephant steps, he searches the kitchen for a pair of scissors, pulling out kitchen drawers until he sees the orange handles on the draining board. He takes one last look, puts his lips to the perfect image, then folds the photograph over, and over, and over into itself.

He begins to cut.

Nick Parker

The Field of Ladders

I

We went to see the field of ladders. I had tired of it after the seventh visit, but Malta hadn't, so there we were again. The ladders are the old-fashioned kind mostly, straight and wooden, with shiny worn rungs from the passing of many feet, starting in the ground, rooted like trees, and going straight up into the sky, where they stop, reaching nothing. Some of the ladders are tall enough to poke at the low-scudding clouds, others barely make it a few feet from the grass. Malta stares in wonder, as she always does, mouthing silently to herself. I watch her lips. Perhaps she is counting the rungs? Once we would have come here together and laughed, given the ladders names, drunk cider in their shade and found beauty in their awkward angles of leaning. Now Malta wanders off alone and the thought of cider makes me queasy and when I try to name a ladder the best I can do is 'Matthew'.

Malta returns from examining a cluster of step-ladders, saying that she thinks she likes the short ones best, they seem contented, and the view from the top doesn't make you dizzy, and they remind her of a friendly uncle she used to visit as a girl. She's wrong of course. The tall ladders are best, and I say so: I say I find their sky-reaching soothing and optimistic, that going as far as they can go is what a ladder should do, and that the short ladders are distasteful to me, with their stumpy and pointless efforts. They are slack ladders, I say. They should put more effort in.

Malta sighs, goes over to a very tall ladder, which is moving slowly in the breeze, and touches one of its lower rungs. Yes, she says, maybe you're right, the tall ones are rather peaceful. All of a sudden I find my feelings are reversed:

I see without doubt that the short ladders are indeed squat and friendly, like they know they could have gone higher but have chosen to take things easy. It's not like there's anything up there to reach, they're quite obviously saying. They are casual and pragmatic ladders. Whereas the tall ladders now seem presumptuous and arrogant, with all their skyward thrusting.

Don't be ridiculous, I snap. Where do they think they're going, huh? Those tall ladders need to get a sense of perspective, I say. I realise that Malta is looking at me. She is mouthing to herself again.

We stand a while in silence, while the shadows of the ladders gradually lengthen in the evening sun. How has it come to this, I think, disagreeing over the height of unreaching ladders? At the same moment, we both notice that in a far corner of the field, at the foot of a medium-sized ladder, a queue of people has gathered. Let's go and look, Malta says, tugging at my sleeve like a child.

We join the line, and wait patiently. Malta seems contented. After a long while, we are at the front of the queue, at the foot of the tallest ladder in the field. I watch Malta's lips again. This time I can tell what she is saying: Just the right height.

She turns to me. You stay here, she says.

I I

We know what they call us when they think we're not listening. They call us the Ladder-loons, or the Rung-nutters, or worse. They forget, of course, that we have with us at all times highly sensitive recording equipment, so sensitive that if we position our microphones correctly, we can hear the fibres in their clothes creak as they breathe. So picking up a half-whispered insult at two hundred yards is no problem to us, even if it is mouthed behind a cupped hand. Latimer says we should ignore these insults. He says people are just jealous of the things that we hear.

Our microphones aren't switched on to monitor cruel words, though. Our microphones have a much nobler purpose. We use them to record the songs of the ladders. When the wind comes in from the East, funnelled by the ridges of the mountains, it blows through the ladders in complex ways, and they give out the most beautiful keening sounds. The tall ladders (which we call 'Hoffnüngs') give out pale and soft notes, notes which induce swooning.

Latimer says they are like baby oboes calling for their mothers. The small ladders (which we call 'Cobbetts') give rise to deep, clear tones, which Latimer says is how the moon would sound, if only we could run out a boom long enough to record it. The ways in which the winds eddy and swirl can make several ladders sing together, so that the air folds over and over itself in great breathtaking swoops of ladder-song. Sometimes we come here intending to set up our equipment, only to find that we can do no more than sob at the beauty of it all, and we have to use the spongy bits off our microphones to wipe away our tears.

Occasionally we argue about which we like best, the sweet sounds of the Hoffnüngs, or the rich tones of the Cobbetts. We can never agree. And what is worse, when we play back our tape recordings, mostly all we get is a sound like static and twigs – just tiny rasps, and the over-amplified clatter of leaves. This is distressing to us because, as Latimer says, if only more people could hear the ladder-song, the world might be a better place, by a rung or two.

Latimer is of the opinion that the ladder-song is the sound of the ladders communicating with each other in a musical tongue. We are of the opinion that perhaps, at times, Latimer can be a bit of a rung-nutter himself. Tonight he has climbed up a Hoffnüng with a cello strapped to his back, and he means to wait for the storm-winds, when he says he too will talk with the ladders and thereby learn their secrets.

We have run out the microphones in readiness. We anticipate quite a performance.

I I I

The fire-fighters said afterwards that yes, they had received a call saying there was a woman who looked as though she was about to jump. They said it had been difficult to make out exactly what was said, on account of a terrible racket going on in the background. Those who had heard the call said it sounded like oboes perhaps, although some say they also heard strings.

The fire-fighters said that it was funny, really. They had rushed there in their engines, and had made haste running out their telescopic ladders, only to look around and realise that their ladders were seemingly surplus to requirement! You had to laugh, they said.

Nick Parker

Although they added swiftly; no, stopping for a quick laugh about the ladders in no way compromised their performance as a rescue service, and couldn't possibly have accounted for what happened next.

The fire-fighters say it wasn't like she jumped, exactly. It was more like she just decided to let gravity take its course. They say yes, it is indeed highly irregular that although she was observed taking to the air, she seemingly did not hit the ground.

The fire-fighters concluded wearily by saying no, whatever the nutter with the cello might have said afterwards, the wild and curious wailings were definitely not emanating from the ladders themselves, and however closely you might listen to those tapes, they in no way suggest that the disorientating crescendos had somehow thickened the very air around her, and buoyed her up, and carried her away on a strange and beautiful lattice of sound.

Kate Ansell

Service Station

The snow fell, and the world pulled over. At Junction 12, they were lucky enough to find a service station: fish and chips, Danish pastries and grainy coffee.

Joe said he needed a wee, so his mum took him to the loo, the disabled one because it was urgent and there was a queue at the Ladies. Louise and her other brother, Patrick, ambled to the on-site shop, aiming to find a copy of *heat* magazine. 'Shit,' she said to him, 'shit, we're in the middle of fucking nowhere.'

And it was true. No one could remember when there'd last been so much snow, and all of it had fallen within fifteen minutes, an act of God for those that believed in H/him, up to your knees, the tops of your thighs, your chest, your neck, your nose, if you were short enough, the tip of your tongue. Louise and Patrick's dad had always been a cautious driver, sixty miles an hour down the motorway, left-hand lane, seatbelts on and sunroof closed. He'd pulled over almost as soon as it started raining, sheets of the stuff, like driving through plate-glass.

They'd found a parking space, and Louise had chased her older brother into the services, arguing about whether she was allowed fish and chips, while her mum carried Joe on her shoulders and Joe was crying because he needed the loo. Then the snow, a sudden blaze of white, burying houses, burying cars, burying men and toddlers and dogs, and claiming the guinea pig that lived in a hutch in Louise and Patrick's back garden, but they didn't know that then. So conclusively was Junction 12 cut off from civilisation that all there was to do until someone dug them out was go and buy *heat* magazine and drink Diet

Coke, and hope that your mother would want an easy life and allow you to eat at Harry Ramsden's in spite of the fact that your doctor said that you ought to think about losing some weight.

Brian had ordered his fish and was drumming his fingers on the Formica tabletop. He was waiting. The young woman behind the counter had explained that she would give him a pager and cook the fish and when it was ready his pager would buzz, and he should come back to the counter and claim it. He'd hated her for having a Brummie accent. Every woman in every service station across the land – all the ones that weren't Scottish – had a Brummie accent. It pissed him off. A Welsh accent he could cope with. A Scottish one he actively enjoyed; it was sing-song, like a mermaid. A Mancunian accent made him laugh. Geordie intonation reminded him of good sex. Listening to Home Counties girls was like eating a bowl of fresh gooseberries. It was only Brummie accents made him want to leap out of the window screaming. Maybe he was being a touch unfair. The thing was, he wanted a cigarette and there weren't any cigarettes to be had.

'There's a service station at Junction 12,' his girlfriend had told him. She was at home with the baby. He'd been up in Middle England visiting his senile aunt for Christmas. Daisy hadn't wanted to take the baby, and frankly he didn't blame her. Neither had he; he hadn't wanted to go at all. He'd half expected to get there and find that she'd died and her annoying yappy terrier had eaten her face.

So Daisy didn't go, and neither did their first-born son. Brian had to go because, if he didn't, he'd feel terrible about it. Daisy had felt a bit terrible on his behalf so she'd lovingly – lovingly! – prepared a route plan for him, marking places of interest and places to stop. She'd told him he ought to stop at Junction 12 on the way back because the fish and chips there were particularly good.

She hadn't told him it was non-smoking, but then he hadn't told her he wasn't a non-smoker. Just because he wasn't smoking around her or around their kid didn't mean he wasn't smoking at all. In fact he'd been taking detours on his way home from work just to suck on some nicotine. After three months of not smoking because she was pregnant and six weeks of listening to Baby Beethoven CDs instead of Eminem, Brian had become so desperate for a cigarette that he'd gone to a faraway café and bought three packs of twenty, highest tar percentage he could find, and chain-smoked them two at a time until he'd drunk all the coffee in the building and they'd sent him home to Daisy, and Daisy had accused him of seeing someone else because he'd been gone so long, and was acting so tense, and had changed into a clean shirt and was using aftershave and chewing gum to cover the smell.

He pulled a packet of Marlboro Red from the lowest pocket of his combats and fingered the cellophane as if it were a coy lover. He got as far as pulling at the gold strip that tore the plastic that encased the cardboard that cushioned the cigarettes that sheltered the tobacco that released the nicotine that...

'Sir,' said somebody with a Brummie accent, 'sir, excuse me, I'm sorry, but you can't...'

'I know,' said Brian, and put the packet back in his trousers.

Patrick was trying to work out if he could reach Junction 12's stock of girlie mags, and whether he could get one to the till without his sister noticing. The place was heaving. Louise was in the opposite corner of the shop, examining some sinister cuddly toys. He stretched as high as he could manage, vertebrae at full tilt, reached up with his right arm and leapt, actually leapt, for the magazine closest to him. In one beautiful gazelle-like action, he obtained the publication, stuffed it up his parka, landed back on the floor, and found himself leafing through football magazines.

Louise crept up behind him. 'Paddy,' she called, with more affection in her voice than was usual, 'do you have ten quid?'

It was a gift. 'I'll pay,' he told her. 'Get yourself a Kit-Kat as well, we're going to be here a while. Tell you what, go to the coffee stand and get everyone a hot drink.'

She began to protest but he gave her a ten-pound note and told her she could keep the change. She handed him armfuls of sugar-based snacks and teen magazines. She left; he paid. Life was beautiful. When he went to look for his mum and dad, he found his dad on a bench by the entrance, watching the snow and looking at the clock. He remarked that mum and Joe had been gone a good while, and sat down to eat a strawberry lace.

Brian was more than a little annoyed. His fish pager hadn't buzzed. Everyone apologised; no one let him smoke. 'We're busy, you see, it's the weather. It's unheard of.' He decided to go for a walk. He could feel the box of fags clinging to his leg like a limpet, like one of those beggar children he'd seen in Delhi, just not letting him go. He played a few games of Space Invaders, and one with a plastic gun where you had to pretend to be a soldier. He went to the shop and bought some Liquorice Allsorts, a copy of *The Sun*, and a weird cuddly sunflower for Daisy. He stood by the window and watched the snow and thought he'd call her. When he did, the baby was crying and she said she'd call him back.

He ate the entire bag of Allsorts and read the paper. He waited for her to call and she didn't. He touched the lump in his trousers, traced the cardboard edges through the material, and tried to act nonchalant.

He spent some time admiring his trousers. They were hand-stitched from parachute silk, and he wasn't entirely sure about them. Daisy'd got them in the sales. Parachute silk! Waste of time. Once, he'd wanted to be a skydiver. Never happened. Too dangerous. Too expensive. His pager buzzed and flashed and he raced up the stairs two at a time and presented it to the Brummie woman who was standing behind the fryer. 'Sorry,' she said. 'We're out of fish.'

He banged his fist on the counter, and she jumped back a little.

'Sorry, sir. It's the weather. Never seen the like, we haven't. Normally, we have a delivery, but what with all this snow, and that.'

He reached for his cigarettes, ripped off the cellophane, and broke the seal on the box. He could smell the tobacco. He had never felt closer to God.

'I'm terribly sorry, sir,' said the woman, 'this is a non-smoking restaurant.'

'Yes,' he replied, placing a cigarette in his mouth and sucking. 'I'm not lighting it.'

It occurred to Patrick that maybe he could find somewhere to enjoy his magazine if he pretended he was going to look for his mum and Joe. Anyway, the magazine was creasing underneath his parka and every time he moved without extreme care it crinkled audibly. Louise was beginning to notice. He said he was going to look for Joe and mum. Louise gave him her empty coffee cup and told him to throw it away.

He went to the Gents, but it was flooded and smelled of piss, and he didn't much fancy tossing off in there. He climbed up three flights of stairs and tried to use the one by the fish and chip restaurant. There was a pretty girl of about Louise's age behind the counter. She smiled and explained that the lavatories were for patrons only. He smiled back and she gave him a bag of chips that someone had left, but said he couldn't stay or she'd get into trouble because they were low on potatoes. He touched her hand as he took the greasy bag, but left without even asking for condiments when he noticed the magazine protruding from his parka.

At the bottom of the stairs, he saw a sign for the disabled loo. He thought that would be a good place to go, so he sat on the stairs and ate the chips, and licked his fingers, and made sure his reading matter was secure. Then he followed the big green arrow.

When he got there, there was a bit of a commotion. He could hear a kid – he thought it was Joe but he couldn't be sure – screaming from inside. Outside the door, there was a young blonde woman in a wheelchair; she was red in the face and swearing a lot. In between swearing, she was talking to a tall man in official green trousers who seemed to be in charge but didn't look much older than Patrick himself. He just kept apologising to the woman, and she kept swearing, and it looked a lot like he didn't really know what to do because he hadn't been expecting anyone disabled to get so cross with him they swore.

There was another man outside the door, holding one of those sinister smiling sunflowers. He was also swearing, but he didn't seem to know the disabled woman. He was clutching a cigarette lighter and scowling. A second man in green trousers was holding a packet of cigarettes and explaining patiently that it was a disabled toilet, not a smoking room, and surely he understood that it was a non-smoking building and he could not smoke. The man made a snatch for the cigarettes but the green-trousered man held on to them very tightly. And then the man screamed 'CUNT!' so loudly that Patrick heard Joe begin to cry through the door. He was sure his mum would probably have fainted or something.

One of the men in green trousers said that, on balance, management felt it would be a risk to allow the gentleman access to his cigarettes. The gentleman stomped off up the stairs muttering obscenities.

Patrick started to talk to mum and Joe through the door. Mum said Joe had done something to the lock but they weren't sure what. Now they couldn't unlock the door. They'd called the fire brigade but the fire brigade couldn't get there because of the snow. Patrick said maybe he could kick the door down, but his mum said he couldn't. He went to tell his dad what had happened, and his dad just said, 'Oh,' and went on looking at the snow and the clock. There wasn't much more he could do, really.

Brian walked up to the fish and chip counter and demanded the chips he'd left there fifteen minutes earlier. The Brummie girl went bright red and told him it was company policy to throw away unclaimed foodstuffs after ten minutes.

His phone rang. It was Daisy. Daisy said the baby was still crying, but she really needed to talk to him because she knew something odd was going on, and she wasn't sure she wanted to know what it was. He asked if she was breaking up with him, and she answered, 'I don't know'. So he asked again, and she answered, 'Yes,' and started crying in time with the baby. He hung up and told the Brummie that she'd better make some more chips.

Patrick had abandoned his pornography to the fire escape. He'd tried to throw it out of the window, but none of the windows would open, and none of the doors either, so he left it just inside the emergency exit. He was never going to get any privacy. Still, he needed kicks. He wandered into the restaurant to look for that pretty girl, just as the gentleman who'd had his cigarettes confiscated was shouting at her. His mouth was so close to her face that spittle was landing on her cheeks.

'What do you mean there are no fucking potatoes?!' screamed Brian. 'The potato famine ended in eighteen-fucking-fifty-two, and that was not in Birmingham, that was in Ireland!'

Louise had just polished off a plate of chips. She turned and saw Patrick and grabbed him because she was scared.

Brian had snatched a plastic knife from the cutlery tray and was waving it in the face of the girl behind the counter. He was talking very loudly and very slowly, like somebody dying at the end of a Shakespearean movie. To begin with his face was pillar-box red, but the colour slowly drained as he spoke until it was white like snow. 'I...Just...Want...Chips,' he said. 'Just... Chips' It became a chant. 'What does a man have to do around here to get some nicotine and a bag of chips?' And he melted to the ground, limbs flailing, groaning like someone on the point of orgasm, high-pitched and self-indulgent and gasping for air.

He crawled along flat to the table where the cutlery tray was resting, and pulled it over so that he was showered with white plastic spoons and forks. He bit into one of them and it snapped, so he took another and it did the same. Then he shoved more and more into his mouth and started to chew. The snapping and crunching set everyone's teeth on edge. Louise closed her eyes and scrunched up her face. While she wasn't looking, the girl ran from behind the counter and grabbed Patrick's hand and squeezed tight.

With eyes like saucers, they watched as Brian peeled off his trousers then, mouth still full of plastic, combats above his head, took a running jump and hit the window at full speed. It smashed in his wake but he kept going, kept running in mid-air, onward, onward, until finally the momentum left him and he landed with an undignified plop in the snow and sank. When Patrick and Louise and the fryer girl ran to the broken window, all they could see was a deep hole in the shape of a man and a pair of combat trousers dangling from the branch of a tree.

Sally Foote

No Dancing Allowed

ast night I did a new etching. I'd been sitting at my kitchen table leafing through a book of Edward Hopper paintings, my fingers through the handle of a coffee mug, the remnants of the paper spread out around me. The light faded and I plugged in a lamp, opened my sketchbook to a new page and drew the pub at the end of my street. The green one. With the mosaic-tiled floor and unmatched tables and chairs. The smooth, dark wood and tea light candles on the tables. You must remember it. It's still the same; well no, it's less busy. A new one has opened up across the road.

I drew a man, sitting on a stool at the bar, reading. And before I knew it he was wearing your black jeans and those old brown moccasins that you've walked in so long you kind of step over the sides. Your Saturday shoes. I imagined walking into that bar and seeing you there like that, waiting for me.

You were resting your elbows on the newspaper, one hand holding back the hair off your forehead. And you were sitting on the stool just like you do, a bit too far away from the counter, with your heels up on the crossbars and your knees wide apart. You had your pint glass perfectly positioned so that you didn't even have to look up to reach for it.

I drew the hair around your ear and the watch on your wrist, and then I touched you on the shoulder to say hello. It's so long since I've seen you. You looked up and smiled, stood too quickly. The newspaper slid off the bar onto the floor and we both bent to pick it up. 'Sorry,' I said. You kissed me hurriedly on each cheek and asked me what I'd like to drink. You leaned over the bar to order, folding your newspaper at the same time. Wrapping it up on itself, rolling and folding, and then stuffing it into the outer pocket of your bag. I hated that you're so rough with things like that. You used to fold the page corners of my books and bend their covers. Now, when I pick them out of the bookshelf, I know that you've read them.

I had my coat in my hand. You took it from me without asking and hung it on the hook next to yours.

Of course, neither of us knew where to begin. I smiled. 'How are you?' I asked. And you smiled. Your finger went round and round a knot in the wood of the bar. I remembered you tracing on my skin and held onto the edges of my chair with both hands.

I hatched in the wallpaper and the rest of the floor, added flowers in a vase, an ashtray further along the bar. I told you about my new job and going diving in Egypt, asked about your dog and what your friends were doing. I gave you back a cufflink I'd found in an old handbag and I reminded you of the wedding we'd been at when you wore it. Your suit had been too hot and my dress had been too tight.

Then, in the corner of the bar, I drew a girl, dancing, with a glass of red wine in one outflung hand. I gave her long, straight hair falling around her face. She was looking at her shoes, one heel lifted off the floor. We stopped talking to watch. I drew the barman waving at her to sit down. There's no dancing allowed in there. They've even got a sign behind the bar saying so, can you believe? We never got dancing right, did we? I hated the spectacle of our mismatching, banging into one another, stepping on your toes. This bar was our neutral ground. You did not ask and I did not decline.

I put my pencil down and rolled it backwards and forwards beneath the palm of my hand. Clickety, click, clickety-click. I looked at you sitting there alone at the bar, in your black roll-neck jumper, with the empty stool beside you, and I started to cry. I pictured all the empty spaces I'd made when I left – the passenger seat in your car, the left-hand side of the bed, the second toothbrush holder above the basin. And of course I wasn't crying for you; I was crying for me.

I said, 'I miss you, I miss you', and, because I didn't want to look at you, I hung my head and the tears dropped onto my skirt. I know what you would say. You'd remind me that I was the one who left you. And that you've moved on. That you're seeing someone else now. I know, I know. I put my hands up over my face. And you'd say wasn't I so much happier now; didn't I remember how I'd always been crying. 'But I'm still crying,' I said out loud, laughed, and leaned back in my chair. I made myself a cup of tea and stood drinking it at the window. Outside the wind had picked up and I could see the silhouettes of the trees shaking against the pink night sky. I opened the window to hear them better.

When I turned back, there was the drawing, with time slowed right down, the moment turning like a coin on the bar, and me waiting to see which way it would fall. I turned the pencil round and, with the eraser, made a small round bald patch on the back of your head. And then to finish, on the left-hand side, I added her hand pressed against the glass on the outside of the door, pushing it inwards. I gave her long fingers, with careful nails.

I traced it all upside down onto the waxed metal plate, scratched out the lines with a fine-pointed pick. I filled the large white tub with acid and dropped it in, holding the corners with my rubber gloves. After it was washed and dry, I rolled thick black ink into the folds of your clothes and the shadows between your fingers. Then I laid the plate face-up on the press, draped the soft, wet paper on top, and turned the crank of the handle to push it through. When I peeled back the paper, there you were, sitting in the pub at the end of my street, reading, a coin on the bar and two coats on adjacent hooks.

Kay Sexton

Acorns & Conkers

'I tell you, the tumble dryer was unusable. It was full of bits of conker and acorn, and the smell was indescribable! They said they thought it would be a good place to hide their treasures, like squirrels do. Kids, they drive you crazy. Mind you, if I hadn't been half-asleep, I'd have seen them in the drum before I put the washing in.'

I'm not listening to Liz; I'm watching Anya. Four years we've been coming to this yoga class – Liz, the homemaker, Anya the shift-working call-centre manager, and me, the freelancer. Liz hasn't noticed the change, but I have. Since Liz's third child arrived, Anya and Phil have been trying to have a baby. Trying and failing.

'Carol, I'm begging you, take my three brats for the weekend and I'll shower you with gold!' She's joking with me; she never lets her darlings out of her sight.

Instead I allow the image of Anya showered in gold to ripen in my mind. Anya with her narrow hands turned up to catch the molten, glowing rain, her small, high breasts dripping with gold, droplets slipping from her neat pubic triangle to meet the widening pool of liquid shining between her long thighs. I catch Anya's eye and hold it. What can she see in my gaze? Whatever it is, she blushes faintly and looks away. I smile. I can be patient.

Liz is oblivious to the effect of her words and my glance.

'Conkers and acorns,' I say. 'Isn't it strange – kids love things that have no value to adults. Do you think they're smarter than us?'

Liz shrugs. Anya looks quizzical, although she won't quite catch my eye.

I continue. 'We reach a point in life where we think things have to have purposes; the purpose of a chestnut is to make a good pudding, the purpose of a yoga class is to keep fit, the purpose of sex is to make babies.'

Anya is hanging on my words, but I stop. Let her do the work now.

'So ...?' she asks.

Not good enough, sweet Anya. Work harder. I simply smile at her.

'Why are children smarter, Carol?' she has to ask. I've given her no choice; the line about sex and babies is a hook into her heart.

'Because they prefer conkers to chestnuts, games to food, running around to yoga.' I let my eyes drop to her neat breasts and watch her nipples tighten under her T-shirt. There is a pause, just long enough for her to breathe in and breathe out, before I finish. 'Just as we should prefer love-making to baby-making.'

Liz sniffs. As a mother, she believes children are the most important thing.

I lift my eyes and watch Anya. She is breathing faster now. Even after four years, she doesn't know how to deal with a woman like me, a dangerous woman. But something in her mind is tilting; she's seeing a different future, one in which being a mother might not define her. In the space of this new future, I am waiting.

We let Liz pull ahead; she has to pick up the baby from the crèche. Anya is colluding with me, slowing down as we get ready to leave the gym.

'Come and have lunch,' I suggest, thinking of my cool, narrow bed on which I can imagine her displayed like a harvest festival. I am no longer able to be patient.

'Okay,' she says, without looking at me. I smile, pulling on my winter coat, feeling the smooth curves of the conkers in my pocket.

Frank Goodman

Tomorrow May Rain

I leave Rhys lying in his own puke because I am too out of it to do anything else. I have to focus hard to stop the room slipping away. I stand up – that's all right. I've just enough left of what they call sense to check that his airways are clear and he's breathing deeply, then I split. The bartender's pissed off with me I can tell.

'He's just some guy I met in the Hofbraukeller,' I lie through slurred lips and shrug.

The shrug goes wrong, the shoulders go up and down too far and I feel myself falling backwards. A table stops my complete collapse. I take a stumbling sideways shift at the street, dreading the first breaths of air – all that good clean oxygen shaking hands with the alcohol, like good old pals, saying, 'We've got the fucker now, mate, let's circulate'. I guess I've got about twenty minutes before I pass out. If I manage to go the right way I might just make the hotel. The might is well optimistic though; my focus is shallow, squeezed close, just lights, pavement, walls. I try to remember the way we came but it's hopeless. It could be any street, any city. I think I've forgotten where we are, which country even. I sit down in a shop doorway with a heavy thud. Then the spinning begins in my head like I'm on a fairground ride going much too fast. I shake my head but that just makes it two rides, one going one way, one the other. I try to get up again but my balance is all shot. What a state, I begin to laugh, what a state.

When I wake up it's still dark so I don't know how long I've been out. There's this girl standing over me, shaking me. 'Nick, wake up.'

At first I don't recognise her, only hear this thick-accented English and feel her hand on my sleeve. I sit up and leave my brain somewhere below me on the pavement. After a while it follows, sliding back into place with a sudden wave of nausea.

I try to focus on the face as she tries to get me up. By the time she has succeeded, so have I. It's the girl from the Polish band playing at the ZIM club, the ones we'd gone to watch the other night before our gig. We'd been introduced between sets – Greta or Gudrun she was. She puts my arm round her neck and I can smell her perfume. It's a nice smell, not hard and chemical like some. She smells of soft towels and warm rooms.

'Thanks, Greta,' I say.

'It's Gerda,' she replies and we wander unsteadily off up the street.

The town is old, cold and silent, full of weary grey facades and little cobblestone streets that should look quaint but somehow only manage to be small. I try to recognise them. 'Might be this one,' I say to Gerda. She turns to the left. 'Then again it might not,' I add and we return to the street we were on.

'What's the hotel called?' Gerda asks, but I have no idea. It's not that I've forgotten – it's that I never knew, never bothered to look, but I know it's on a street full of shops selling pianos. I tell Gerda this but it doesn't help. I concentrate harder on the streets. It's not that they don't look familiar; it's more that I recognise them all, somehow, somewhere, from some place or another. I begin to think that we may be really lost but then we turn into a square full of ragged plane trees and grubby, brooding statues of gaunt-faced men. The hotel is just off this square, but I still can't remember what the town is called. I ask Gerda. She tells me. It doesn't ring a bell.

I stop her by a shop window full of marzipan sweets and heart-shaped bread. I lean so close my breath steams up the glass. I point out a row of figures walking past a marzipan house with pale white marzipan faces and bright, coloured bodies. She pulls at me to come on but I hold her there and make her look. There's a fat man who's obviously the mayor and a band with a large marzipan drum. There are soldiers in neat rows, marzipan guns shouldered, marching in time. It's a triumph of good order.

'Look,' I say, 'there's a whole world just waiting to be eaten.'

Then I draw a facsimile of the bread heart in my window breath and write 'Gerda' in the middle. Gerda smiles and shakes her head. I'm feeling more in control of myself, like I've come up out of paralytic and back into drunk, walking down this dark street in bugger-knows-where, Eastern Europe, the World, with a blonde girl who smells nice. I feel ragingly happy and start to sing. After the first verse, Gerda joins in and it occurs to me that this girl can really sing. Not like those 'come see me wiggle my tits and ass' warblers that front up most circuit bands, you know, the ones that sound like they've got tissue paper stuck up their nostrils and are worried it'll come out during the performance.

'You're a good singer,' I tell her.

She smiles. 'I'm the best, the bloody best, you know.' Then she laughs like there's some personal joke.

We reach the hotel and stand outside like lovers at the end of a date. I'm on a roll now; my night has been reborn. 'C'mon up for a drink,' I say. 'It's too late to go home.'

She looks at me and shakes her head. 'After all you've had, I should think you'd want to sleep it off.'

'I'll sleep when I'm old,' I tell her. 'In fact, I may never get out of bed then.'

She looks at me with her big dark eyes. 'People living like you do don't get old too often, I think.' She smiles ruefully, not critical, just weary.

'I know that,' I say, making her big-eyed face back at her.

She looks away then, maybe a little irritated.

'I'm glowing like the metal on the edge of a knife, glowing like the metal on the edge of a knife,' I sing over and over again like on the record.

'Okay, okay,' she says, smiling in mock pain. 'You're crazy, okay, you qualify, right.'

I think she's about to leave but then she turns and walks into the hotel.

The good thing about these hotel rooms is that they're so cheap that the band members get one each. There's nothing worse than spending six months on the road with the belching and farting rhythm section who, no matter how disgusting you become, can always go one better. That said, it's not much of a room, with wallpaper the colour of stale bread and a big iron bedstead (somehow the word bed seems inappropriate) that creaks like an old park swing. Gerda takes off her coat and drops it on the only chair. She's still wearing her stage gear, the tight, shiny black pants and loose mauve chiffon top.

'So where's this little bottle, Nick? I hope it's not Romanian, a truly shitty drink from a truly shitty country.'

'Nah, don't you worry,' I tell her, 'we insist that Lance ships out four cases of something suitably Scottish for each tour as part of the deal.' I reach beneath the mattress and pull out the bottle, then I wipe the smears off the two glasses on the bedside table and pour her half a glass.

She says, 'Don't be stingy, baby – you know that movie?'

I fill up the glass, laughing. Gerda sits down on her coat and props her legs up on the chair arm. Her silver lamé stilettos are mended with masking tape underneath. She puts one hand behind her head and drinks with the other. 'Here's to Lance,' she says. 'Lance is the fat man, yes?'

'Yes, Lance is the fat manager all right. Here's to Lance's Scotch,' I say.

We raise our glasses and drink. My throat is sore after all that beer but the first swallow burns it numb and the second is just fine. It's still dark outside, though you get that sensation that morning is creeping up somewhere, in the texture of the darkness or the stillness in the air, like something old and animal in me knows the night will soon be gone. Gerda waves her legs in the air, humming to a tune that's in her head. I ask her what it is she's singing and she tells me that it's an old Polish folk tune that was maybe written by Chopin, but it's hard to know as almost everything gets attributed to Chopin in Poland. She tells me the song is about a young woman who got lost on a mountain while searching for her lover and died there. The song says that if you go to the mountain and call out, you'll hear her calling back to you hoping that it's her lover calling.

'Very sad,' I tell her and ask what happened to the lover.

Gerda takes off her shoe and wiggles her toes. 'Oh, he got back safely. The men always do in such songs.'

I say I didn't know there were any mountains in Poland.

'There aren't,' she replies. 'That's what makes it so sad.'

Gerda gets up and opens the window. The night air wafts in but it's no fresher, only damper. She leans out and looks up at the big church opposite. 'Look at that bastard thing, will you, so big and smug and old? Do you know what it says to me, Nick?'

'You're going to tell me anyway,' I reply.

'It's saying I am important and you are not, so you must do as you are told. All fucking big buildings are saying this I think. God, this place is so much like home it makes me want to throw up. Cold places, clouds, fucking snow when it should be warm, and everywhere history, old people, old buildings, staring, glaring. I see the look in their faces, arrogance, disdain. What for? For God's sake? What have they achieved other than to belong to some crappy little country that rips itself apart every thirty or forty years then puts another statue in the square?'

She turns back to me, her eyes a little wild, mascara smudged like she's been rubbing it. 'Where I come from everybody leaves or is wanting to, you know? Shit, I left home to get away from places like this and now look at me.' She shuts the window, shutting out the night. 'It's all going wrong, Nick. It's all going wrong, isn't it?'

'It went wrong a long time ago,' I tell her. 'There's no other way it can go now.' I shake my head knowingly. I shake it too much and start to get dizzy again. I feel sorry for her in the same way I felt sorry for myself when I finally recognised the crock of shit that was my lot. My hands so full of nothing I could hardly carry it all.

Gerda shakes her head too, shakes away what I have said. 'It should be like in the movies.'

I laugh at that.

'Why not?' She points a finger at my disparagement. 'People know what they want life to be like, don't they? They make movies about it, all the time.'

'What, like Mary Poppins?'

She ignores me, lost in some private inner monologue. I wait for it to surface. She puts her arms round my neck, still holding the drink, and I smell that soft smell again but now mingled with a malt edge.

'You know what? I love the movies,' she says. 'But I don't always watch the actors, oh no.' She waves a finger in front of my nose. 'I watch what's behind them. Big places, rich places, warm places, and I think this is my place, wherever it is.'

'It's nowhere, that's where it is,' I tell her.

'Then maybe that is my place, if you say so, nowhere.' She kisses me lightly, so lightly that at first I'm not sure she's done it. 'You ever played the Gulf, Nick? Nothing but shitty desert, but boy is it hot and the money is great. Two years we were out there. Two years of no Poland, no snow, no queuing for every stupid little thing. Then the Chinese bands came, working for bloody nothing as usual and they had all these little girls in Lycra with no tits and tiny asses. The Arabs liked them 'cause they looked so much like boys, liked them even better than they liked blondes.' She finished her drink and held out the glass. I filled it.

'So you must come from Liverpool.' She grinned. 'All British bands are from Liverpool, I think.'

'That's a load of bollocks,' I tell her. 'Silly bloody European stereotyping.'

'Oh!' She pouts at me. 'Where are you from then?'

'Well,' I tell her, feeling a bit of a prat, 'Liverpool actually.'

She laughs and taps her head, which gets me laughing too.

'Will you go back to England, Nick?' she asks suddenly. 'Will you go back forever one day?'

It's a question everybody asks me sooner or later, like it's important, like if they knew the answer they would have a key piece to the jigsaw of my life. Or maybe they're just curious and I'm paranoid. It's one of those questions I stopped asking myself some years ago. 'Home is wherever I happen to be,' I tell her. 'Any bloody city will do: Kiev, Riga and Sofia, Tallinn, Bratislava – even bloody Minsk, bring 'em all on. "I'll never walk down Lime Street any more,"' I croon. 'Though I suppose the song should probably now go, "I'll never walk through Lime Street's pedestrianised shopping precinct any more."'

'Don't you go home even to see your family?' she asks, surprised.

I don't like these conversations. They always end up sensible and ordinary, so I stop it in its tracks. 'They're all dead,' I lie.

'Oh,' says Gerda, 'I'm sorry.'

'Don't be,' I tell her, 'I'm not.'

Gerda leans forward and buries her face in my chest. She isn't becoming drunk exactly but the Scotch is bringing out something within her, like chemicals develop an image on paper. She looks up at me with those dark eyes, now even darker. There's something about her that makes me want her and yet not want her, like if I screw her now, she'll merge with all those other near-forgotten nights in towns like this, where all I've got left is the trace of a smell or the fleeting memory of a touch.

I put my hand underneath her chin and I tilt her face up so that I can take a long look. I try to remember everything, the way her tousled fringe droops across her forehead, the colour of her eyes, the shape of her mouth. Even as I look I feel it slipping away, losing focus and I know she's going to elude me too. She looks back at me just as hard and I realise that she's thinking the same.

'So, where do you go from here?' she asks.

'Somewhere south,' I say. 'Bulgaria or Croatia.'

'Not many clubs down there. It'll be all concrete gyms and assembly halls with tinny PAs and endless calls for "All you need is love" and "Satisfaction".'

'What about you?'

'North, worse luck.' She shakes her head. 'Moldavia and bloody Belarus.'

'We were there last month,' I tell her, 'lucky if you get a bleedin' PA at all – but it wasn't snowing there.'

'It doesn't matter,' she says flatly, 'places like that act like it's snowing all the time.' She taps my brow. 'Snowing in the head.'

Gerda takes another sip from her Scotch then puts the glass down and begins to unbutton my shirt. I want to stop her but I don't. I want to tell her that I want to tell her something important, but I don't know what it is. I only know that the more I talk to her, the nearer I seem to get to it. Sometimes it seems so close, late at night, early in the morning, at times like these it seems so close, but there's never enough time, the night never lasts long enough, or the conversation ends, or I become too drunk to know what anyone is saying any more. She unbuttons my belt and thrusts her hands down inside my trousers with a little sigh, and I know the time for conversation has passed.

Soon we're naked and I'm laying her backward on the edge of the bed. She's very pale, pubic hair, armpit hair, all wispy and blond. She lifts her legs to facilitate my entry. No time for foreplay. The night is almost over and it's too late for whatever secret sweetness there might have been between us. Gerda closes her eyes and drifts off into whatever movie is playing in her head, leaving me alone in the cool, damp room. Over her shoulder I see that the sky is growing white behind the church. The spire is gnarled and twisted like an old root against the sky. The years it must have looked on at happy, lonely, ephemeral scenes like these. I lean over and kiss Gerda again because I've never felt as alone as I do now, like the vast spaces of my life are all cold and open before me. I always knew I was going nowhere, I just thought it would take me longer to get there. She wraps her legs round me and smiles, safe, for the moment, in her dream.

Soon the sun is bright and high. I watch Gerda dress and feel a little better. She is a pretty girl, a nice girl, far too nice for me. I paint a little future for her, which is rosy and quite absurd. Far away from a skinny Liverpool-Irish guitarist with a fractured history and a damaged liver.

She finishes dressing and turns to me. 'Will you come and see me at the club tonight?'

Her smile is so honest and open that I just stare at it, caught for a moment in the simplicity of the thing. 'Of course,' I say.

She kisses me and slips out the door. I watch her from the window though I don't let her see me watching, watch till she is a tiny figure at the end of the street. Just before she goes out of sight, she turns and waves like she knew I would be looking all along.

It's then and only then that I remember we're leaving today.

I run after her in wheezy gasps, down the stairs and across the lobby, out into the bitter morning street. When I get to the corner all the roads are empty, just a couple of taxi drivers slumped asleep in their cars and a scruffy cream bus full of old women in black. I stare at them angrily because there's nothing else I can do. They stare angrily back. It's then that the tiredness sets in. I'm so tired that I can hardly stand, so tired that it's like the whole weight of the sky is just lying down on me. My mouth is full of bile and the first jabbing pains of dehydration are lancing up behind my eyelids. So I go back to the hotel and lie down on the bed and am still asleep when Lance brings the van along the street and toots the horn.

Sara Hiorns

All the Hairdressers I Have Ever Been To

1. **Late 1970s. Mr Giuseppe, Kingsbury, London NW9**
Called 'Mr Spaghetti' by my enlightened grandmother, Mr Giuseppe was typically ebullient and so nice to me that I was afraid of him. He would put a board over the arms of his cutting chair to raise me to adult height. His salon was very old-fashioned and when I first had my hair cut in a bob (circa 1978) I had to have it dried under one of those space helmet dryer things. I wondered why everyone kept laughing when I spoke until my Mum told me I was shouting over the noise of the dryer. I thought the bob made me look like the girl with the blue-framed specs in the year above me at school.

2. Early 1980s. Hazel, Causton Road, London N6
Hazel had a salon room in her own home. She was a boss-eyed, extremely sentimental Jewish woman with a colostomy bag, who told me that Barbra Streisand was 'her God'. She had found love late in life and was desperate to have kids, which was difficult due to her medical condition. Eventually, after some kind of fertility treatment, she had twins and appeared on the cover of *Woman's Own* without her glasses on. I cannot remember what she used to do to my hair, but it can't have been anything sensational. She once told me that when I was grown up I would be an eccentric, which I thought was rich coming from her.

3. Mid 1980s. Erjan, Crouch End Broadway, London N8
I cannot remember the name of the salon where Erjan plied his trade but it was opposite Budgens and, I think, still functions as a hairdresser's or something

similar. Erjan was a camp Turk with a sticky, curly perm. He always asked me from the ages of 11 to 15 whether I was taking my exams soon. He was also friendly with 'an actress' called Jackie who lived in our flats.

4. Late 1980s. Suzi, North London

Suzi was a hairdresser who used to come round to your house and rinse out your shampoo with a measuring jug over the kitchen sink. She was a very jolly, pretty London girl whose business card had a big pair of open scissors on it. She once got off with a greengrocer from Muswell Hill who would bring loads of produce round to her house on Saturday evenings. Suzi was connected to other people in our lives (maybe one of them recommended her), including the oddly named Gary Paradise, all-round diamond geezer, who lived in our flats, and Ruth, an alcoholic who worked with my mum whom we used to call 'Fanlight Fanny'. All of a sudden Suzi took up with an old flame and wanted to settle down. She put us in touch with another mobile hairdresser called Joanna who was very New Age and got on everyone's nerves with her talk of runes and Reiki healing and the like.

5. Early 1990s. Clipjoint, University of Sussex Campus

This was another mobile concern, run out of a toilet in a hall of residence on Sussex Campus by a wild-eyed Irishwoman. The whereabouts of the clipjoint was signified by a life-sized cut-out of Humphrey Bogart that had an A4 piece of paper sellotaped to it on which someone had written 'Clipjoint' in biro. I went there because it was cheap. The woman used to do my hair in what she lovingly termed a 'Purdey cut' after *The Avengers*, I suppose. Twice I took with me boys who were too shy to go alone. First Robert, studying engineering, who the mad Irishwoman said was 'a handsome bugger'; then Roy, host of 'Rockin Roy's Radio Show' on University Radio Falmer. He wanted his long rocker's hair sorted out because he was after a woman.

6. Early 1990s. The Greenhouse (I think), Imperial Arcade, Brighton

My first experience of a really trendy hairdresser's, where, to my lasting mortification, I had a terrible coughing fit and everyone looked at me. One of the girls doing the sweeping up had to get me a drink of water. They did my hair very nicely in this place and made me look like Martika (remember her?), at least that's what someone said, though it was expensive and the style difficult to maintain. There is very little else to say about this place, other than it was where I first observed that trendy and/or expensive hairdressers are no good if you are hoping to overhear an interesting chat or a good story.

7. Early 1990s. Salon 22, East Street, Brighton

This was the place I went to after walking round Brighton about three times wondering whether or not to have my hair cut short. I chose Salon 22 because it looked friendly and not at all cool. They fussed over lots of magazines with me. My hair was cut very well by Maureen: a well-preserved Scot with a long honey-coloured bob who wore Barbra Streisand trousers, liked going to the races and lived in Kemp Town with a man called Kenny. I told her that one of my flatmates, a young man called David, worked in the liquor aisle at Kemp Town Safeways. She took to going in there on her way home and striking up suggestive conversations with him. In the end he took to hiding behind the fire doors whenever he heard the swish of her trousers. Later on, my hair was cut by a wide-eyed girl called Alison. Salon 22 was a sleepy place. You did not always need an appointment.

8. Early 1990s. Somewhere in Watling Avenue, Burnt Oak

I cannot remember the name of this place, or the hairdresser who did my hair. I do remember that they always tried to make me look as though I had a spiral perm and were very pleased with themselves when they had managed it. There were always people sitting around pontificating (one a fat bloke) who had nothing to do with the hairdresser's. One of the girls had five kids all by different men.

9. Early 1990s. Hairdresser's in DH Evans, Wood Green Shopping City, London N22

I had my hair done by a stroppy girl who seemed very bitter about men. I also once decided to push the boat out and had my nails done by a big-haired Greek Cypriot girl, who made me put my coat on before she painted them because a woman had complained earlier in the day that putting on her coat had smudged the varnish. This was an uneventful place.

10. Mid 1990s. Ahead in Style, Crouch End Hill, London N8

Ahead in Style was run by two gay blokes (Keith and Steve, not a couple) from

Norfolk who had amazing Norfolk accents. Steve once told me a story about his mother getting trapped in his shower cubicle, 'Because she couldn't stoop to open the door when it was jammed.' She'd had hysterics and from that day forth would not shower without Steve in the room. Another time, Keith engaged me in a long and very involved discussion about cures for psoriasis, a condition from which I suffer. One of these was drinking potato juice: a friend of his had tried it but had to give it up because the taste was so vile. Most people say the word 'vile' in an ironic way but Keith said it very seriously and he kept on repeating it in his Norfolk accent. I found this hilarious but had to try not to laugh because, obviously, he could see my face in the mirror. At one point the lads acquired a surly Chinese trainee whom they called Mr Ki and teased mercilessly.

11. Mid 1990s. Hairs R Us, Holloway Road, London N7

This was one of the best hairdressers for stories and general all-round good fun. I can't remember the name of the woman who did my hair but there was another girl there called Fionnula, which I always thought was a good name. Hairs R Us subscribed to the theory that the salon is one big conversation and everyone chipped in their two penn'orth. There was an Irish lady called Mary whose visits often coincided with mine, who was a housekeeper for a local priest. She would have her hair dyed jet black, lacquered and coaxed into a huge beehive around which she would tie a blue chiffon scarf. When her hair was done she sat on to talk and drink tea. She wore white plastic shoes and had very veiny legs. Once my hairdresser told us a story she'd read in the local paper about a Greek Orthodox priest in Palmers Green who'd had an affair with his housekeeper, then tried to murder her to cover it up. 'You'd better watch out, Mary, your geezer might get ideas about you!' she said and everyone roared with laughter. Mary was offended and didn't turn up for a while after that. At Hairs R Us they used to cut my hair very nicely in a kind of sixties-style bob. And it was cheap.

12. Late 1990s. John Dennis, London WC1

This was a more expensive place than I was used to but some posh girls I was working with recommended it and I grew to like Gill who cut my hair because she came from the same part of London as me. The place was named after the owner's dead father who appeared to him during a near-death experience (he nearly fell off a ladder while putting the finishing touches to the salon's decor a week before opening). The girls at this salon had some of the biggest arses I have ever seen and wore extremely inappropriate clothing for girls with arses that size. They all said that they went to the gym regularly but I found this extremely hard to believe. Although the girls were really nice, John Dennis bordered on the posh and didn't have the knockabout quality of Hairs R Us. Though, when I was pregnant they all had words of wisdom for me, especially Kylene who did the shampooing. She told me that her mother had been exactly the same shape as me when she had her brother and that I would definitely have a boy. My daughter is nearly two now.

13. 2002. Cutting @ 149 Brick Lane, London E1

Trapped in Whitechapel by a small child, I had to find somewhere nearby and didn't fancy the place on Vallance Road, which was the size of a coal shed and as exposed as a goldfish bowl. I must say they cut my hair splendidly here. Many people commented on this at my 30th birthday party but it was just too poncey and I didn't feel they were interested in you unless you were a model or a conceptual artist (they organise art exhibitions in the basement from time to time). My hairdresser, Richard, sneered at me when I said I thought going to Noodle King in Bethnal Green was a good night out. 'I like the bars around Hoxton Square,' he said.

14. 2003 - present. Hairline Junction, Wakefield Street, London E6

I got off to a bad start here. When I first went in on my birthday last year for a cut and blow dry, I encountered the rudest, scariest Essex girl ever (skinny, sunbed tan, aggressive gum-chewing). She yanked my head about all over the place and as I had a terrible headache it was an awful experience. For some reason I got it into my head that I had to tame her, so I went back to have my grey hairs dyed. I asked her, while she was doing it, whether she would cut my daughter's hair and she said to tell my boyfriend to bring her in while the dye was taking. My daughter melted her heart, not only because she is cute but also because she didn't make a fuss during her haircut. 'She was so fucking good,' swore Jo, plying her with sweets. After that she was friendly towards me, telling me all about her wedding, how she couldn't have kids etc., etc.

Then, recently, I went in to find she had gone. 'We ain't surprised,' said Hazel, the owner, sucking in her cheeks. I got the impression that Jo was a bit of a pariah, and so were her customers. When I went in just before Easter Teresa did me and I joined in with the ribald laughter as a Pat Butcher-style woman who worked in 'Bootses' told filthy jokes. I then joined the debate about whether the enormous shampoo girl should have a tattoo on her toe ('Already got one on me left tit') and was finally invited to Faces in Basildon on a night out. 'Isn't that where Leah Betts took that ecstasy?' I asked. But it turns out that was a place called Racquel's.

Marek Kazmierski

Wake

Middle of the night, you gently shook me awake. I asked what was wrong and in a half-conscious voice you explained you'd woken for some reason, watched me for a while, couldn't see or hear me breathing. You said you'd been overcome by a swell of fear. Fear that I'd died in my sleep. You'd wanted, needed to check I was okay, and, having done so, you mumbled goodnight and dropped straight back into dreams again.

Afterwards, I couldn't get to sleep myself, shocked by your calm-as-fuck explanation for waking me. You'd imagined I'd died next to you, but, seeing I hadn't, you'd just left me to my own thoughts. Then, a few months later, you left for good.

But that was later. The next morning, you made the whole 'dead' thing seem funny. You said it was just a midnight freak-out. Dreams getting out of control. Though sorry for spooking me, you didn't think it was the least bit serious.

I laughed along at the time, but I don't see it that way now. Can't forgive myself. How could I not see that you should've embraced, should've kissed me at least? Made some display of relief before leaving me alone in that bed again. Left me with more than a half-lit smile to go on. Told the truth. That we were passing each other in the night. Literally. Woken me earlier.

Lewis Hall

Trash

Thursday 12/02/04, 2.06 a.m.
Nosferatu shadow-fingers scuttled across the skirting board and onto the skinny carpet. The fingers spindled and stretched to demonic length. Another shadow merged with mine granting my shadow-creature a Luciferic beard. I had a smoke of the joint and watched a faint plume of shadow-smoke fume from my shadow-demon's jaws. My new stereo span out Goldfrapp's 'Black Cherry' to me and my creature. My brain began to chill and I knew the shadow-demon was also pretty stoned as neither of us had spoken for a long time. My housemates had gone to bed hours ago. I missed having someone to pass the joint to and the demon wouldn't take it.

I staggered off the couch; I had to put the bins out before oblivion smothered me. My mind rode fairground teacups, slowly spinning, as I moved about. Wrenching the bin-liner from the bin took a lot out of me. I tied the top of the bin-liner. It was all taking too long. My left hand bumbled up the bin-liner containing my battered old stereo; half was left uncovered. The back door was a fucking bastard; only a particular push-and-handle waggle could coax it open. I put down the bags to work at it.

Outside, raindrops kamikazied their way to my head. I'd gone out in just my T-shirt and the rain punished my stupidity. It was cruel but it smelt so much cleaner than my smoggy living room. The bin area, however, stank of sour milk. I dropped all the bin-bags over the waist-high back wall as swiftly as I could. Water rolled off those that had been left in the backyard, dribbling over my hands, arms and shoes. My stomach mumbled that I should get back into the house as quickly as possible and get out the Jaffa Cakes. My eyelids nodded in agreement and gently whispered...bed...time.

Thursday 12/02/04, 9.00 a.m.
The 'William Tell Overture' roused me from the womb of my bed – I always set the alarm on my phone to play the most brain-bashing tunes. That way, I'll either get up or feel suitably punished for my extra lie-in. Dressed only in my dressing gown, I slipped on my trainers to survey the bin men's work. Rain had painted the concrete of the yard a darker shade of grey. My genitals dangled under my gown, enjoying the cool air they rarely got to experience.

Twats! The stereo had been tossed back over the wall. Why were the bin men so picky? They would take a tied bag of plate-scraped leftovers, used condoms and even decapitated monkey heads, but a stereo in an untied bag offended their sensibilities.

I'd not replaced the lids of the outside bins and now water swam around their bellies. I tipped them over; my legs received a pre-shower shower. The day was already on the verge of bad and it was still early. I picked up the council bin-liners that the bin men had left. They were really soggy.

Wednesday 18/02/04, 9.17 p.m.
The whole ground floor carried the stench of greasy meat, like a burger van at a football game. 'Lemon Jelly' softly strummed, bleeped and sound-bit from my stereo while Jenny, curled up on the sofa, rambled on about her boyfriend's bathrooms. I was on the chair in the corner of the living room, hunched over a plate of oven-baked burgers.

'It's really weird' – Jenny's nostrils flared like a bunny sniffing for danger – 'they're both right next to each other. Tin's room' – she referred to her boyfriend Martin as Tin – 'is by the family bathroom. Then there's his sister's room.' Her little hand gestures indicated the relationship between the various rooms. 'Then, like right opposite his sister's room is a bathroom with just a toilet, shower thing and a sink. It's only really used by guests.'

I bit into my artery-clogging dinner, causing tomato ketchup to dribble out the sides of the bread and stain my fingers. I wished I was actually doing something, but I felt more at ease in the house with Jenny. If I was outside, my hair would have to be waxed up, people would expect me to burp out random statements, be jolly, prat around. Out there, I wouldn't allow people to watch me gobble sauce-dripping slabs of grease-patties.

'It's decorated like a jungle and it even has a cuddly monkey in the corner.'

'Like Finders Keepers?' I began to take an interest.

'Yeah, like Finders Keepers.'

As a kid I'd loved the idea of that television programme. The programme itself was shit but the idea...wow. Running around, ransacking a house looking for clues. As Jenny carried on about the other bathroom, I wondered if burglars my age had watched Finders Keepers as children.

I put my plate down on the floor and Jenny's face froze. I understood, picked up my plate and went to the kitchen to clean up. By not using any words, she'd given me a chance to be tidy and feel good about it. The bin-liner, however, hadn't been put in the bin properly. I had to wade my hand through sloppy goo till I found the liner's end, crumpled among the rubbish. I pulled and an empty two-litre bottle of Diet Coke doused in tikka masala dropped to the kitchen floor.

With the bin-liner finally inserted, I used a wooden spoon to scrape burger fat from my baking tray into the bin. Masochistically, I lifted my hand to my nose. The spices of the masala couldn't mask the stink of rotting meat. I set the bag by the back door, rolled my shoulders, cracked my knuckles and gave the door a glare. It opened first time – perhaps I'd finally got the knack. I slammed the bag over the wall, ripped the other brimming bin-bags from the outside bins, and sent them over too, chucked the shattered stereo out of my yard and then spat at the wall. Sometimes I felt very angry and didn't know why. I didn't punch the wall because I didn't want to hurt my hand. My rage only went as far as the spit. I'd failed to phlegm with enough vigour and had to wipe loose slather from my chin.

Thursday 19/02/04, 8.47 a.m.

I hadn't been able to sleep so had opened my window in the night. A gust of morning wind had sent my blue-suited Day of The Dead figurine diving to the floor. Luckily, it woke me up, snapping me from a futile sex dream starring my ex. Cool morning air had filled my room and made me shiver as I tumbled out of bed. I got dressed without even showering. I put on yesterday's boxer shorts and smelt various pairs of socks from my floor till I found a set that didn't reek of dead feet. Outside, I collected up the council bin-liners and realised the stereo had been returned again. Fucking cocks! I'd have to cover it up next week.

Wednesday 25/02/04, 10.27 p.m.

I really needed a wank. I wasn't quite hard yet so I still had time to hunt down some true masturbatory material, but that required more energy than I could muster. Fortunately, my wank-bank was heaving with flashes of the week so far: the brunette in front of me in the queue for Liquid, the queue bunched up tight, the hem of her tiny kilt-skirt stroking my cock through my jeans; my ex wearing high boots, a bitchy glare and a twinge of a smirk as she caught me staring at her cleavage; typing my essay while Lyndsey pretended to sleep, her bare shoulders bobbing above her duvet.

I scanned my DVDs. Fifteen of them, the majority 18s, yet barely a nipple among the lot. I used scene access, one-hour thirty-eight minutes in. I ran the film at half-speed. With my trousers and boxers draped around my ankles, I dropped back onto my bed, resting on my left elbow. Susan George was stripped and her ordeal had just begun as my right wrist frantically pumped. I thrashed until I felt a burning surge then eased off, thrashing and relaxing, thrashing and relaxing, my arse muscles tight together, until Susan George's nipples were at their peak of visibility. Squeezing kilt-girl's arse and slipping my hand round to feel the warmth of her cunt; a quick hard fuck with my angry ex, her leather knee-highs still on, my teeth pressed against her neck in a vampiric kiss, her hair gripped in my hand, my cock to the hilt; my kissing head pushing Lyndsey's duvet further down. I milked my cock briskly, circled cum over the dry skin of my bell end, and leant off the bed, my dripping hand searching. Yesterday's sweat-stiffened socks soaked up my mess.

The rape continued on the television and I felt a bit sickened. I really needed to sponge all the madness off my brain. I needed to shower. I had to take the bins out first though as I wouldn't be in the mood to steep myself in more filth afterwards. This shower was going to be really good; all my muck was going to drown like parasites in a flea bath.

I tilted my head back and took in Orion, the Big Dipper and Pegasus. I didn't know any other constellations. Few lights polluted my backyard. The stars always made me feel better. They put things into perspective. Jews in

Nazi concentration camps must have looked through the mists of incinerators up at the stars and felt they could have been anywhere. People thousands of years ago must have looked up and found comfort in the watching gods. Distant friends and relatives and those I missed saw the same stars. My ex always said that if I was in a good mood then it'd be a starry night, but that was bollocks. The stars are consistent and unaffected by the volatile moods of a bunch of stupid animals on one small planet.

The breeze woke me up. I had an extra bin-liner in my hand. That stereo wasn't going to dodge the dump this week. I fumbled to find it amongst bustling bags. Gunk licked my arm. That shower was definitely needed. At last, despite partial blindness, I found the stereo bag. I covered the caved-in speaker, which peeped out of its liner, with the fresh bin-bag, then placed the stereo over the wall. The other bin-bags I slung over. My neighbours were old ladies, too deaf to pick up the racket.

Thursday 26/02/04, 9.09 a.m.

I slept well, covers snuggling my fresh skin, and got ready for university very quickly. With my uni bag tossed over my shoulder, I went to view my empty backyard. They had actually taken the stereo! Finally I'd managed to smuggle it into the back of their truck. The bin men, however, had had their revenge. They hadn't left us any council bin-liners. Our last one had sacrificed itself to ensure the stereo's destruction. I was not happy.

Wednesday 03/03/04, 7.52 p.m.

The Doors demanded that I show them the way to the next whisky bar, they said not to ask why. I wanted to find a few bars myself that night. My wallet was heavy and eager to lighten its load. Its weight, however, was pure coin; it had been stripped of paper. But I was still going to lather myself in as much luxury as I could muster. I began by attaching a fresh Mach 3 Turbo blade to my razor and creaming my face with Asda shaving gel. After ripping all the ginger-tinted hair from my chin, cheeks and top lip, I was starting to resemble myself for the first time in a while. I washed Allure over the smooth skin, relishing the aftershave burn, and dabbed it behind my ears and onto my wrists. Oozing with confidence, I even made a scent trail from my belly button to my starving crotch. The aftershave smelt like Benidorm 2001 – that was where the two of us had first melded to become a team.

With so little cash available, scientific mixing was the key to inebriation. Over the bathroom sink, I downed a repugnant vodka-and-red-wine shot. My body attempted to reject the mixture but after a couple of painful stomach gips it conceded to my hellbent will. Using my ex-girlfriend's toothbrush, a trophy, stolen, I scrubbed wine stains from my teeth. The bristles, after a month in my possession, had begun to splay but they were still much healthier than those on my own brush.

Matt trotted downstairs, retroed in '70s-style fashion robbed from the charity shop for a bargain price. 'Let's rock and roll.'

Before my rocking could kick-start, however, the rubbish had to be dealt with. In the kitchen I tugged the bin-bag free. I did this with my shirt sleeves tightly rolled and with the bin at arm's length. The bag was released with comparable ease. Trash juice trailed behind me as I made my way to the back door. We'd had to purchase our own bin-liners and their quality seemed doubtful.

I shook the back door open and jumped outside. The Bolognese-milk-brine trail continued out into the backyard. I popped the bags over the wall with an eager vodka thirst then hopped back inside. A tea towel made a half-arsed mop under my foot.

I returned to the bathroom to dry out my bladder for the night ahead. The bathroom bin was spilling over. I gave my cock a single shake then stuffed it away again. A man at a neighbouring urinal had once explained to me that anything more than two shakes was a wank – this had changed my life irreparably. I tied the bathroom carrier bag, shoved the back door open and heaved the bag over the back wall into the alley. It hit the wall's top, dropped, split, and scattered our bathroom waste over the yard.

'Go, go, Johnny, go, go,' yelled Matt.

I shut the back door. Urine had dripped from my cock and made a wet patch in my pristinely ironed Calvin Klein's. Luckily they were black. I walked jacketless into the winter night – cloakroom queues are obscene – with two shirt buttons undone and damp boxer shorts.

Thursday 04/03/04, 11.36 a.m.

I knocked back two pints of dusty tap water. The first sleeked down my gullet like mountain spring water. The second had a distinct metallic after-burn. As

I gulped, my seminar tutor would be starting his usual spiel to my group. If it hadn't been for drinker's dawn and morning glory, my head would still have been plastered to my pillow. I slipped my trainers on and grabbed the dustpan and brush. A painful ten minutes of gathering rolled-up toothpaste tubes, naked toilet rolls and balls of miscellaneous hair, ensued. The bin men had left us six bin-liners – jackpot.

Wednesday 10/03/04, 6.29 p.m.

I opened my front door for Lyndsey and followed her in. My demeanour gnarled when I caught sight of Matt slouched on the couch. Lyndsey sat down next to him.

'I'm going to start cooking,' I told Lyndsey as my eyes stabbed Matt's skull.
'Do you need a hand?'
'No, I'm alright, it's only pasta.' But I did really want her to come and help. I did really want her. I did really want her to come.

Matt strode into the kitchen. 'What time does the play start?'

I shrugged, and mumbled half seven.

There was no door between the living room and kitchen and I could see Lyndsey twisting strands of her hair together as she watched The Simpsons. While I tipped dried pasta shells into a pan of water, Matt pulled the bin-liner out. I laid two chicken breasts on the grill as he lugged the bin outside – he was trying to make up for not pissing off quicker.

To ensure precise domestic science, I bleeped my Casio stopwatch into count-up. Twelve minutes of pure boil till the pasta achieved adequate consistency. Ten minutes till Lyndsey should make a girlish sniff with a look of surprise and say, 'Mmm, that actually smells nice.' Nine minutes till the chicken and bacon should be diced and added to the pasta sauce. Eight minutes till the Sainsbury's Italian Herb sauce should start its simmer. Seven minutes till the bacon should be rotated. Six minutes till I should dryly spout something witty. Five minutes till the bacon should join the grilling chicken. Four minutes till the chicken should be flipped. Three minutes till Matt should return from taking out the bins. The rest of the time would be given over to improvisation and innuendo-laden talk.

In the end, however, conversation took second stage to The Simpsons double-bill and dripped more with inanity than innuendo. My wine glass emptied too quickly while Lyndsey's seemed resistant to her stingy sips. Two minutes and twelve seconds in, Matt returned. 'I'm off to work on my essay, have fun guys.' He saluted us both and gave me a sly wink that made me shudder. The pasta took four minutes before even beginning to boil, the chicken forgot to tell me to flip it, the bacon's crispiness crumbled to charcoal, and Lyndsey's 'Mmm' of gourmet-expectant pleasure became a puzzled 'Urmm, is something burning?' My dry wit was perhaps a little too dehydrating and improvisation was more akin to chaos and panic. These became the dominant themes of the eighteen minutes till I served up the food.

Thursday 11/03/04, 9.42 a.m.

After a morning wank fuelled by images of Lyndsey's sleek, streamlined legs and her tight arse, I nimbled outside. Our rubbish still sat in the yard. Matt had somehow failed but worse than that: Hitchcockian birds had raided during the night. Our bin-bags' stomachs had been pecked apart and their innards scattered across the yard. I suspected either of the two main beak-wielding air-vermin: the nonchalant pigeon or seagulls from nearby Morecambe Bay. Those absolute flying fucks!

In the far corner of the yard, leaning against the back wall, lurked a tattered bag signed with still-moist bird plop. The bag covered the top half of a hefty hunk of junk; a second liner covered its base. Through tears in the thick black polythene I made out the contents of the two bags: an old and battered stereo.

Katy Darby

Naughty

They met at a party. His birthday party, in fact; or partly his. Jay and three friends had clubbed together to hire what Maxey had assured them was a teeth-grindingly fashionable underground bar in Smithfield, opposite the old fleshmarket.

'London's very own meat-packing district,' Jay had commented, neutrally, calculating the distance to the nearest tube. None of his friends seemed capable of walking five minutes without getting hopelessly lost, veering into a pub, or simply giving up. Si had called him from the street once, claiming he 'couldn't go on'. When Jay stepped outside to get away from the juddering techno, he recognised Si's squat shape and fawn cashmere from across the street, bellowing into his mobile as he stomped along in the wrong direction.

Jay needn't have worried, in the end. People came in hordes, arriving somewhere between fashionably and ridiculously late, dragging friends, partners and 'the guy I met in Candy' along too. By eleven the place was comfortably full; by one it heaved like a corpseful of maggots. The dance floor resembled the Northern Line in rush hour, and hopping, complaining lines formed outside the toilets as people went into cubicles in pairs and came out sniffing brightly. Nico had panicked about attendance and added '+2' to every name on the guest-list, which was why Jay never worked out who she'd come with, or if she'd simply limpeted onto one of the single blokes in the queue when she saw there was a late-night party at the end of it.

She wasn't drunk when she came up to him, but she was certainly sparking with something other than natural exuberance. Feeling Methuselan and responsible, he'd interleaved his cocktails with mineral water all night and, now the party was winding down and the place was vomiting people out onto the streets in search of taxis, Jay was annoyed to discover he wasn't even vaguely drunk. Perhaps if he'd been more pissed he would've had the courage to pull Zoë from the Art Department, but he'd missed his chance and she'd copped off with some friend-of-a-friend. They were bumping into him even now, writhing unsteadily against the basement railings. He shuffled aside petulantly and stood in line as people, some of whom he recognised, brushed past, aiming kisses at his cheek and yelping goodbyes. He checked his watch: an ingot of expensive diving hardware his parents, at a loss for a present as usual, had bought him.

'Taxi taxi?'

It wasn't the usual nightbird-call of the unlicensed cabbie. He turned around.

'What?'

She stood in front of him in heels like silver stalks, holding a cigarette. 'Got a light?' She flashed her packet. 'Want one?'

'Thanks, no, I don't.'

He made a pocket-patting gesture and, to his surprise, found some matches. The cab queue undulated in front of them in peristaltic slow motion. She didn't seem in a hurry to get one, and he was waiting until the drunken twat contingent left, feeling that his self-restraint entitled him to a taxi to himself.

'You're the birthday boy, yes?'

'One of them, yeah. Jay.'

He offered his hand and she shook it, a boxy handbag swinging from her wrist, tangled up in little glittering bracelets.

'I'm Cam. Friend of Tony.'

He nodded, no wiser. She had nice eyes, dark brown outlined in grey smoky shadow that was beginning to crease into the fine folds of her eyelids. Her mouth sparkled wetly in the streetlight: there was some sort of fine glitter in her lipstick, and it left shining stains on the white butt of her cigarette. He wondered what it tasted like. Zoë had been waving a brace of flavoured glosses under his nose earlier, failing to get him to wear some.

Suddenly she darted right, waving extravagantly at a cab coming down the opposite side of the street. It swerved in towards her and the driver's head emerged.

'Where you going, love?'

She dropped her fag into a puddle, shooting Jay an inquiring look. 'Where are *you* going?' she asked him. He started to shake his head, then glanced at the shouting, number-swapping queue ahead. He didn't want to wait another half-hour; sharing wouldn't kill him.

'Russell Square,' he said, and opened the back door for her. She looked at him with a calculating air as he edged in after her and the driver executed a flashy three-point turn. The orange streetlights flickered through the window like a zoetrope.

'That's lucky,' she said airily. 'I live very near. Just off Holborn.'

'Nice area.'

'Yeah, shit flat though. I share with my brother. Will. And his girlfriend.'

'That's nice.'

'No it's not, she's repellent. All right, that's unfair. She's not repellent, she's just ... off-putting.'

He smiled privately into the vinyl-smelling darkness. He could think of a few people who matched that description.

'I couldn't share again,' he said, realising it was true. Perhaps he really was a grown-up now.

'You know, I got here so late I don't really feel I've begun,' she mused. 'I was talking to this really interesting girl and she just disappeared.'

'Yeah, same thing happened to me but I found her outside, getting off with some random.'

She poked him gently in the thigh. 'Do you want to hang out at yours for a bit?' she said casually. 'I don't want to go to bed yet, plus I could walk home from there in five minutes.'

He glanced at her shoes. 'Even in those?'

'It's a question of practice. *And* I've only got a fiver for cab fare: it'll be more than that.'

He glanced out of the window and watched the sleeping monoliths of the City rush by. Who was this girl anyway? Was she trying to pull him, or was she just lonely, or high, or what?

'Take me back and I'll feed you dogs,' she murmured into his ear.

He twisted around, bewildered. 'You'll feed me *what*?'

'*Drugs*,' she enunciated, tapping a nostril. Her eyes were wide and luminous in the strobe of the passing lights. The cab driver studiously ignored them.

'Oh, what the fuck,' said Jay.

Jay's flat was small and perfect, high in a portered Victorian block within sight of the concrete ziggurat of the Brunswick Centre. Cam had said nothing in the lift, only smiling enigmatically and reapplying her lip-gloss in the tan-tinted wall mirrors. He unlocked the door and they walked straight through into the living room, dark and quiet and citrus-smelling. New lemons gleamed in the rosewood fruit bowl on his desk, and she crossed to them, picking one up and smelling it.

'Nice,' she said. She untangled her bag from her bracelets and put it on the coffee table. It was shaped like a little treasure chest, the handle a chunk of horn with thick silver links in either end. He turned the desk and standard lamps on at the wall switch, creating a moody gloom. She replaced the lemon and raised an eyebrow. 'Smooth.'

He shrugged, pleased, and shucked his coat onto the corner of the sofa, stepping into the kitchen to forage in the fridge.

'Do you want a drink?' he called.

'Sure. What is there?' Her voice sounded high and artificially polite. He felt that they had taken a step back, somehow, and that perhaps he would find himself spending the next few hours talking inconsequentially about mortgages or the job market. He yanked the freezer open fiercely and was relieved to find a bottle of vodka.

'Vodka, red wine, champagne,' he told her, pulling two highball glasses from the cupboard.

'Vodka,' she said.

'Do you need tonic? There isn't any.'

She appeared in the doorway behind him, leaning in an exaggerated noir-vamp pose. 'No. If you have vermouth I can make Martinis.'

'Sorry.'

'With ice, then. Can I smoke?'

'Sure. There's an ashtray on the shelf.' He had one for visitors, and the occasional weekend joint.

When he came back with two cold glasses numbing his hands she was standing in front of his bookshelf, a fresh cigarette burning, staring at the titles with a cocked head and concentrated frown.

'Lots of stuff on film,' she said. 'You're a director?'

'Commercials,' he corrected her, modestly. 'I've done a few shorts, nothing major. No time.'

She picked up a pristine copy of Robert McKee's *Story* – the glossy cover flashed at him under the lamplight as she opened it – scanning a few sentences. He'd always meant to read it. She put it back and came across to him, picking her drink out of his hand. He sat down on the sofa, feeling the leather squish and sigh beneath him, but she remained standing, wandering aimlessly around the room, touching things, ornaments and photographs, as though confirming their reality.

'Drugs!' she said suddenly, and opened her miniature strongbox of a handbag. She pulled out a little square of glossy magazine paper and unfolded it onto the glass coffee table. It was as intricate as origami. She took out a cashcard and her five-pound note from another section of her bag and, tipping out half of the gritty white crystals, began to chop them into rough lines. She looked up at him courteously.

'Shall I do it, or ...?'

He shook his head.

'All yours.' He sipped his vodka, glad to watch her unobserved. She had very dark brown hair, almost black, cut in a longish shiny bob. She tucked one wing of it behind her ear as she concentrated. She peeled off her figure-hugging blue wraparound and laid it neatly over his coat on the corner of the sofa. Underneath she wore a black mesh T-shirt, a shadow of bra visible through it. She caught him looking and smiled. 'For dancing,' she said. 'I get so sweaty.'

She finished arranging the lines and cleared coasters and magazines from the table so that he could get at his share. She rolled the fiver into a tight little tube and offered it to him. It was a long time since he'd done coke. Everyone at the office bored him senseless about how much he was missing, but he couldn't be bothered with the hole-and-corner drudgery of going out and scoring. You never knew what you were getting anyway.

'I have a fifty if you want,' he offered.

She shook her head with a little laugh. 'Doesn't make much of a difference to the experience,' she said, and dipped her face forward over the table, sucking up her line neatly, leaving the glass almost bare, like a magic trick. He took his turn, inhaling inexpertly, too hard, and felt the crystal bitterness melt down the back of his throat. He swigged some vodka to wash away the taste, grimacing.

'Naughty,' he said absently, imagining his mother a silent witness at the scene, and Cam looked up at him with a peculiar, delighted expression on her face.

He put on some music, Billie Holiday, and they chattered for a bit, picking at subjects deftly, like hummingbirds. He found out that she was doing some sort of ill-paid educational publishing thing based at the unfashionable end of Islington. Her bare arms shone like turned wood in the light. Billie sang God Bless the Child a third time; he brought the vodka through so they could help themselves, and it slowly formed a ring of condensation on the glass between them. She wasn't drinking much, he noticed. She had a habit of scooping out the half-melted ice cubes from her glass and half-sucking, half-chewing them.

At some point, when the cackle of dawn birds was beginning to intertwine itself with Billie's cracked yearning, she tipped out the rest of the powder and chopped them two more lines, thinner than before. They took turns, and he could feel his heart fluttering in his chest as it hit. She picked up her card and contemplated it. 'I always like to cut this stuff with a Solo,' she said. 'I may not be able to pay by card at Tesco's, but by God I can buy Class As.'

She grinned up at him and he smiled back. Then, to his surprise, she licked the cutting edge of the card clean before she put it back in its compartment. He winced. 'I don't know how you can do that. That stuff tastes foul.'

She licked her lips, pantomiming ecstasy. 'Mmm. *Delicious* drugs.' She dabbed her finger over the scattering of white grains left on the table top, as though she were picking up crumbs, and sucked it. 'It's an acquired thing. I always think it tastes a bit like come.' Her dark eyes locked onto his, laughing. 'Don't you?'

He wasn't sure how he was supposed to respond. 'Let's just say I wouldn't like to do a blind taste test.'

She stared at him for a moment, as if assessing the length of a leap.

'Here,' she said. 'Try it.' She leaned over and kissed him deep and hard. The warm jolt of her mouth gave way to a delicious cold shock as a sliver of ice slipped between their tongues. She tasted of smoke and coke. When he drew away she had manoeuvred half-out of her fishnet T-shirt, pulling it down to her waist, and he could see the smooth cleft of her breasts and the thin, muscular vertical hollow traced in her stomach down to her navel.

'Let's go to bed,' she said, decisively.

They hadn't fucked until the late hours of the morning, although they'd fooled around in his big, creaking bed for an invigorating, exhausting length of time, and he thought he had made her come with his coke-numb tongue. They slept a little, sprawled half-out of the tangled sheets, and he woke up to see her sliding off the bed. She padded out to the kitchen on naked feet, and came back with a dripping pint-glass of water, tinkling with ice cubes.

'We'll need this,' she said, and made him drink. Her other hand stole beneath the sheets to linger on his groin. The coke-fuelled hammering of his heart had quelled, and he felt himself stirring under her slim hot fingers.

'Shall we give it another go?' he asked. She nodded, hair swinging. They didn't fall asleep again until lunchtime.

They saw each other every few days after that, except when he was working late, editing, in the company's Soho suites. Sometimes she'd walk down and meet him afterwards, letting him take her to the club he belonged to, an after-hours speakeasy consisting of a couple of rooms in a knackered, oak-panelled Greek Street building. They spent a lot of time screwing, but he didn't find her company awkward afterwards. It was something he'd secretly dreaded, barely knowing her and having to find out about her later, in instalments, over cocktails and her eternal white Davidoffs. They talked about all sorts of stuff: she claimed to be shockingly apolitical, but was opinionated nonetheless.

'But that *is* politics,' he insisted, laughing, as she made some point about opera funding. 'You just won't admit it!'

'You can say that about anything,' she countered, twirling her straw. 'Life is politics. Sex is politics. I'm just not interested in politics *as* politics.'

That night she'd pulled a sleeping mask from her bag as they wandered in to the bedroom.

'I can close the curtains,' he offered, although he liked to see the moonlight slip down her body. She shook her head. 'Have you got a tie you don't wear much?'

He pulled one from the rack, a loud silk thing, another hopeless gift from his parents. She smiled and wound it around her hands, snapping it experimentally.

'Great,' she said, pulling him down to the bed and straddling him. 'Do you like to be dominated?' she asked conversationally.

He was momentarily at a loss. Then he nodded. 'Sometimes,' he said. His heart was thudding again, although they hadn't taken anything together since that first night.

'Thought so.' She tied his wrists to the bed's brass bars, so that his hands crossed above his head. He wondered how she could tell. A lucky guess? Perhaps she went for that type – or they for her. She slipped the mask over his eyes and he felt her tongue, warm and wet, move over his collarbone. Her teeth teased his nipple and he felt her lips curve in a smile.

His phone rang. He ignored it, frowning at his edit screen, then looked around the office irritably, hoping for someone more junior to take it. The room was empty – a meeting probably. He sighed and picked up the handset.

'Jay, Commercials.'

There was a long indrawn breath.

'*Hello* darling.'

'Cam? Are you OK?'

'Just *fine*.'

'We're meeting tonight, aren't we? Are you calling to cancel? It's no problem because I've got quite a backlog ...'

'*No*, I'm calling to get you hard.'

An electric shiver stroked his spine. He glanced around again: misty figures strode purposefully past the smoked glass walls, but no one came in.

'*What?*'

'I took the day off. I'm lying in bed, thinking about you.' Her breathing was slow and slightly ragged. He instinctively put a hand up to cup the phone, cover it.

'I'm naked,' she said thickly. 'I've got an ice cube and I'm melting it on my nipples. It's running down my breasts and soaking into the sheets ...'

Her phone-sex phase lasted a few weeks, and he was more relieved than disappointed when she declared herself bored with the game. As he'd explained, it would have been different if he'd had his own office, but ... The next day she'd rung the bell of his flat while he was watching a DVD, one of last year's blockbusters that he was trying to work his way through. He yawned over to the intercom to find her brandishing a black box at the camera. He buzzed her in and heard her high heels clattering on the pine floor outside his door. He opened it and kissed her, ushering her in.

'Got a present for you,' she said, and dangled the box at him, flopping down on the sofa, one eye on the explosion frozen on the TV screen. He sat down next to her and took the box, gift-wrapped in black paper and flimsy pink ribbon. He undid the bow and lifted the lid to find a six-inch candle of clear plastic with a wire coming out of one end. He lifted it and turned it in his hands, admiring the heavy vinyl smoothness. The sunset light from the window glanced rainbows out of it.

'Does it light up?' he asked, tracing the cord to a white plastic battery pack at the other end.

She crossed her eyes at him. 'No, duh, it *vibrates*. Have you never seen one before?'

'Not like this,' he admitted. 'I thought they were more ... lifelike.'

'There's more,' she said, a grin in her voice. She pulled another, larger box from behind her back and put it on the table.

'First things first,' Jay said, feeling slightly intimidated. 'How do I switch this thing on?' She leaned forward and twisted a black dial at its base. The glassy rod leaped to life in his hands.

'Jesus sodding Christ!' he yelled, and dropped it on the sofa between them, where it hummed and burrowed energetically between the cushions. The noise, and the buzz that had vibrated through his hands, reminded him of the first time he'd tried to use an electric toothbrush; he'd been scared then, too. She gripped the blind, nuzzling thing in a firm hand and turned it off. He looked up at her with wide eyes.

'Don't *worry*,' she admonished. 'I'll show you what to do.'

Eventually, he looked back on the toys period as a sort of breather. Despite the regular, expensive trips to the Hoxton branch of Shhh! and his far too frequent and obvious confusion as to the purpose of the instruments she picked out, he'd begun to acquire a certain expertise and enjoy exercising his skills on her when she suddenly began to express an interest in being filmed.

'But why not?' she asked innocently. 'You're a director. You can borrow the equipment from work. Who better to film us? You don't want to get someone else in, do you?' He looked up sharply at that, to see a grin so broad he knew she was joking. He never could tell, with Cam.

'Let's be clear,' he said firmly. 'If we're going to do this, I am *not* borrowing the gear from work.' Her brown eyes sparkled with satisfaction, and he realised that he'd already conceded too much. It was a classic negotiating tactic: ask for more than you need, and settle for what you wanted in the first place.

Afterwards, though, he couldn't deny that the camera had lent a porn-dirty, performative dimension to their sex life. She loved to play up to it, and on the nights she couldn't come over, he loved to watch her twist in Hi-Def on the brass bed next door, her hips bucking and her hair sprawled over the sheets like split black glass.

'Naughty ...' she'd gasp, between gritted white teeth.

A month later, he stared down at the dildo in blank horror. It lay between them on the glass like a dinosaur turd, gleaming black and carved in photorealistic, wince-inducing detail. It was a good foot long and, to Jay's eye, looked like it should be on display at the Natural History Museum as a warning to the wayward, not nestling against a stack of GQs on his coffee table.

'I am *not* sodomising you with *that*,' he said flatly.

She hooked her arm through his and kissed the angle of his jaw. He rubbed his eyes despairingly, wishing they could just forget all this escalating kinkiness and microwave some lasagne and fall asleep on the sofa together, dribbling on each other's shoulders, like a normal couple.

'You don't have to, silly,' she said softly. He was halfway through a sigh of relief when fresh terror shuddered through him as he realised what she might mean. Nothing was ever enough for her, he thought: naughty didn't even begin to cover what she'd persuaded him to do over the last six months. Not that he hadn't enjoyed a lot of it: God no, but this was too much. He couldn't take it any more. He certainly couldn't take *that*.

He bit his thumb viciously. He was going to have to say no, never again, and they'd fight, and she'd leave him and find someone else with fewer hang-ups and an enormous, dildo-sized cock, and he'd miss her and the talking about politics that weren't politics, and going out for dinner and the programmes they always watched together and the regular instalments of

Tales of Will's Off-Putting Girlfriend and the sex, the sex ...

'You know my friend Susa?' she said, stroking his arm as though calming a frightened animal. He looked at her with dumb void eyes. '*You* know, the relationship therapist? Well, she's bi herself, and she sort of expressed an interest in me – in *us* – really, and I said I'd ask you if ... well ... you fancied a threesome.'

She had gone off with Susa in the end, and having spent one crystalline, dreamlike, sweaty night with both of them that would echo down the halls of his memory until he drooled his care-home last, Jay told himself that he'd seen it coming. It had been the lifting of a bittersweet burden; he'd thrown himself into his work and barely reeled back from the brink of getting fired. By the time he'd worked through the backlog of things he should have done and people he should have seen over the last half-year, he found that actually, although there was still a soft hollow ache where she had been, like the space where a tooth once grew, he wasn't as depressed about the break-up as he'd thought he would be.

His friends rejoiced as he came among them again. A select few had been following the saga of the relationship with dropped and sometimes drooling jaws. Jay refused to give her number to Si, although Si insisted that a woman who was sexually high-maintenance was really no trouble. She emailed him occasionally and he saw her a few months later at a party, the black back of her head entwined with Susa's blonde curls. He'd been obscurely pleased that the sight didn't bother him, although it was certainly turning a few other male heads. Anyway, after a few abortive one-night stands, he was seeing Maxey from Graphic Design and it was going rather well. She was eel-slippery and energetic in bed, and he sometimes thought of the black box of toys gathering dust under the dresser, but didn't want to push it. Maxey was a lapsed neurotic, after all.

So he wasn't put out to spot Cam across the room at a big launch party in a converted church in Kensington a year later, standing chatting animatedly to one of the authors' agents. A glass of *cava* tilted dangerously in one hand as she gestured, and a tall, black-haired man – her brother by the look of him – hovered behind her, looking awkward. A ring glinted on his wedding finger; so the repellent girlfriend had got her evil wish after all. Jay glanced around for Susa as he walked up with Maxey in tow, but couldn't spot her.

'Cam!' he said, sketching a little wave as she turned. Her brown eyes, shadowed with grey, widened in surprise and delight.

'*Excuse* me,' she said to the agent – a short, fey-looking blond man, who obligingly moved on to someone else – and surged forward to kiss his cheek. 'Jay!' she exclaimed. She turned to Maxey and offered her hand. 'I'm Cam,' she said with a wide open smile.

Maxey looked blank; Jay had spared her the specific details of their relationship, always referring darkly and only half-jokingly to 'the insatiable one'. 'Maxey,' she said, and then her face suddenly cleared. 'Tony's friend Cam?'

Cam nodded.

'How *is* he?' asked Maxey, and Jay, feeling like a spare part, slipped off to get drinks. When he returned, Maxey and Cam's brother had gone. He stood there for a moment, at a loss.

'Oh *there* you are,' Cam said impatiently. 'Maxey saw Nico go past and wanted to catch up. She said she might be some time.' She took a glass, drained it, and put both her empties on the floor.

'What about, er ...' He was embarrassed to realise that he'd forgotten her brother's name.

She waved it away. 'Oh, he's gone off to get me some fags. I never understand why they can't sell them in churches. It's *been* deconsecrated, and anyway, they're practically incense. Do you want to see the authors' VIP room?'

It was a characteristic lightning switch of subject. He shrugged. 'Sure.'

'It's where all the decent booze is kept,' she explained, leading him swiftly by the hand between crowdlets, 'but because I organised the party, I can get in. Dogsbody's perks.'

She tapped a code into the doorframe of the ex-vestry, and the door swung open. It was pitch-black and she fumbled for the switch, throwing a pale glow over leather armchairs and fruit arrangements.

'Nice, isn't it?' she whispered, turning the bottles on the bar so the labels lined up.

He nodded.

'They come in here after and we all suck up to them and get pissed.' Her lips twisted in a smile. 'If you suck up to *me*, I can score you some Glenlivet.'

He weighed his champagne glass in his hand, suddenly aware that they were in a compromising situation and he wasn't sure how to extricate himself.

'I should, er ...'

She was up in a second, stalking towards him, taking his glass and putting it on a sideboard out of reach. The blood spread warmly through his body like a domestic fire.

'What?' she said, looking at him very closely, her eyes huge and unavoidable. *'What?'* she whispered, leaning in slowly, putting her mouth up to his until their lips were a millimetre apart. He closed his eyes in a yearning agony of surrender.

She stopped. Her breath hushed on his lips. They were not quite touching. He realised with a giddy lurch that she was going to make him do it of his own free will.

He pulled her against him violently, kissing her, breath coming hard. She twisted his hair in her fingers, tugging it to a prickling, pleasurable tautness. His hand crept below her skirt and ruched up the silk, hooking a thumb into her knickers and tugging them swiftly down.

Afterwards they sprawled, gasping like fish on the blue-grey swirl of the carpet. It was like coming off a drug, or booze, or cigarettes, he thought. You could be good for a year, no problems, happy and healthy as never before, and then *blam*. One hit, one slug, one drag and all your good intentions and clean living were flushed down the drain. He was already beginning to feel sorry for poor Maxey. Perhaps Si would ...

She sat up and looked at him quizzically. She reached his glass down from the sideboard and offered it to him. He shook his head against the rug, laughing quietly. 'No thanks,' he said, breathlessly.

She sipped a little, daintily. 'How did that feel?' she asked.

'Naughty,' he said, and smiled up at her.

He didn't know how he'd managed for so long without kissing that hot broad mouth, without seeing her breasts jerk and her black sheet of hair skirl over them when she came. Her dark, solemn eyes searched his as she twisted the glass in her hand so he could see the ring glinting on her wedding finger.

She smiled slowly. 'Me too,' she said.

Melissa Bellovin

Night, Aragon

The discussion went on: what to do with the men. They were gathered on the hill, clustered in a circle. Their hands and ankles were tied, though they didn't need to be; we watched them with our bayonets, which never make a mistake. Their weapons were thrown in a pile in our camp. Their poor, broken ammunition we had discharged and guarded in a secret place, just in case. There was the possibility that more would come, though it was well past nightfall; the moon was high in the sky, the air was cold. But they could continue to come. So it is with these stupid Aragonese. Mothers and children, even, blundering into our territory, asking for salvation. We would have no choice but to kill them.

We had hot water, with which we made tea, and watched the prisoners shivering without their coats, which we sat upon. The coats were poor but warmed the cold ground. This was like mother's milk compared to where we came from, but we were not against some comfort, however small. We continued to discuss the matter.

'We can wait for the women to show up and shoot them all at once,' said one of us.

'We hang each of them from one of the barren trees in the valley. We put a cut orange in each one's mouth, and let the prisoner savour that last taste before we disembowel him,' said another.

This seemed like the only plan because to wait for the women would cost us the night, during which we could begin to advance upon the next town, eighteen miles away.

One of our soldiers tore a bolt of silk into dozens of pieces as he watched the prisoners, muttering numbers to himself. I had not thought to count the prisoners, but fortunately it was being done. Another soldier began to load the rifles we had found in the enemy's camp. We could not afford to use our own ammunition when theirs was available. If there were a misfire, then so be it. One less soul to scratch.

There is one particular thing I wish to describe: the feel of one of the prisoners against me as I dragged him down the hill. Though he was kicking, and the cowardly cries from his chest could not be entirely muffled by the scarf which was meant to cover both his eyes and his mouth – such are the condolences we give one another before the final moment – his arms were cold. Not the cold of a night, but the cold of a corpse. It's true we had already taken their coats, and the prisoner's flesh was exposed through his ragged clothes, but the coldness of his skin – it was remarkable. As I dragged him down the hill towards the wooden posts one of our soldiers had begun to hammer into the earth in the most terrible hurry, I rubbed his arm with my gloved hand, trying to make the blood circulate. I could not kill a man if he was already dead.

Down the hill we struggled, helped by one good Frenchman and his bayonet. At last we tied him to a post. In my hurry to hang the prisoner I forgot the orange, which the prisoner before him, broken and twisted at his feet, had suffered. The air was filled with the stench of the liquids we had extracted.

After approximately twenty minutes the prisoners were dispensed with. We then realised we had no more fuel for light and would have to remain at the foot of the hill until sunrise, or we might not make it anywhere. We drank up the cold tea and watched the clear black sky lose the light until the prisoners were finally in darkness, unlit by the moon, and we no longer had to look at their broken bodies, even from the backs of our heads or through closed eyes, because there was nothing left to see. Not until the sun came up, and we took one last look.

The women had not come. Luckily, others in our regiment were dispersed throughout the valley.

We left for the next town.

The tiredness we felt was insurmountable.

Margot Stedman

Flight

In the dream I can fly, eagle-steady as I circle and plummet and ascend again on updrafts of sparkling light. It is *my* dream, perfect and secret and out of the reach of interfering hands. As I soar, my cry spills on the wind, which sprinkles it all through the forest in the valley below.

In my dream there is nothing to be afraid of. There are no shadows: just silver-blue coolness and calm and whatever pleases me. The voices can't find the door to my dream, though they try, I know they try. When I hear them on the outside, tap-tapping as they search for a crack in the sky to seep through, I stay as still as silence, until they go their muttering way.

Do you know the voices? They make me talk like this – I say: 'Would you like a cup of caterpillars for seven years on the table and round we go away on diamonds and apples because ghosts will get you now Tuesday's always tomorrow.' The words gush out like from a burst dam and they don't tell me where they've come from or where they're going. They smash everything in their way and sometimes I feel like they'll drown me. But eventually the dam's exhausted and they trickle to an end.

The voices weren't always there. There was a time when one thing followed another, when life had a shape and people didn't change in front of my eyes. I know there was a wedding day because I've seen the photographs, felt the veil, smelled the man in his aftershave and smiles. And there was a baby, two babies, rabbit-pink and goldfish-mouthed in their search for food and I *did* feed them. They smelled of powder and milk and sometimes shady grass on summer afternoons as I snuggled my nose into their piglet warmth and let them breathe for me.

If you promise not to tell the voices, promise to let me know if you hear them coming (they will come), I'll tell you about before.

*

First I'm twenty and I smile as I marry and I'm a farmer's wife. Just like that. My days are oceans of wheat where the wind rushes over the surface like a spirit and makes the crop ripple and swell. I am young. I have an apron and responsibilities. My husband has a tractor and work, so much work to do. The mornings scorch my skin and bleach my unaccustomed eyes because I am not from here. There is space, so much space in the paddocks that stretch over the horizon, out to the red of the desert's edge. Sadness flutters inside me without explanation.

My husband has sun-browned skin and dark eyes and loves me. I feed him, tired and sweaty at midday as I drive to where his tractor is. (Did you hear? The voices said 'Stop it! You know what we'll do if you tell, Miriam. Stop talking!' But I won't stop talking. Not yet.)

My husband loves me and holds me at night and tries to blow away the sadness like blowing dust off my shoulders. He wishes me better and we mustn't tell anyone because I'm probably just tired.

And my babies are born. My husband's finest crop, he boasts, and he loves them too and they become Matthew and Sarah. (You see? I do remember.) They grow big enough to crawl among the geraniums in the sandy garden and tear off flowers like savages. Sometimes they eat them and pieces of petal drip red from their glistening mouths. They gaze at one another as if in a mirror and each delights to find the other's grin. We all delight in these days of shimmering laughter and easy shade where I plant an orchard for the future. I defy the climate and bury things from my past in the crumbling soil: peach trees, pear trees, an old kind of apple. Nectarines and pomegranates. I water them every night as the crickets sing and the stars rain down in profusion around the Southern Cross.

One day a snake appears, brown and persuasive, just near the babies on their rug. I scream but my husband doesn't see it. It disappears before he can kill it, though he fetches the gun from the house just in case. But no need.

In the evenings pink cockatoos screech their way across the sky in crazy silhouette and smoke hangs in the bushfire air blown across the plain. The sun brands the horizon a fierce orange and soon it's dark and cooler for a while.

(In my dream there is water and snow, and mountains covered in pines, which make the breeze whisper as they nod to one another. I am invisible as I hover above them.)

So I am still young though life is harder and drought rasps at the door with its arid tongue and almost eats us all up. My husband shrivels somewhere inside as crops fail and hope withers under the relentless blue.

On a neighbour's property the baby dies from a spider bite and I take my little ones to the funeral. The church has a tin roof and bakes in the morning light, which streams though the stained glass onto the tiny white coffin. We sing, we pray, and when the priest isn't looking the coffin lid opens and the spider emerges in the shape of a baby with too many legs and watches me with all its eyes. People chant on, oblivious, but I cannot look away and I know that the spider will come for my children one day.

Because my husband loves me I say nothing and the rains come briefly as lightning cracks the ghost gum by the gate. My orchard licks up the water like a thirsty cat and blooms and fruits with the help of the wild bees.

The spider baby with its rough black hairs and dark, shiny fangs is heavy, like a real baby. I know because once I woke to find it sitting stony-still on my back, listening to me breathe. That time my husband chased it off for me, and took me to the doctor, though I hadn't been bitten so I wasn't sure why. The doctor had a watery smile and gave me tablets that made my tongue move too much and the children laughed and copied me, enchanted by the new silly game.

The spider baby began to follow me. It watched me from the trees in my orchard, from the top of the windmill that drew the water up from the bore, from under the table in the kitchen as I made bread and butter for the children. I hid it from my husband, who had been left scarred inside by the drought.

The nasty voice scolded me and told me dreadful things. It first arrived one gloomy Thursday when clouds rolled in heavy from the south and sulked but wouldn't cry. But after a while the other voice joined it. It was the other voice that showed me the way. It understood that I had to save my little ones from the angry, hungry spider baby. 'Miriam, my darling, it will all be alright,' it said. 'I'll help you. Everything will be alright.'

It's sunset at the dam my husband built for the livestock, and a crow barks its disapproval from a dead jarrah. A dragonfly is floating on the glassy surface as we wade in. The children squeal with pleasure as the water runs its fingers over their goose-bumps, tickles their tummies so that they cover them with both hands at first. I know that they will be safe here, as I hold them tightly, feeling their plump skin rub against me. I shiver. Droplets stick their long eyelashes into clumps. He has a runny nose which sends a trickle down his lip and into his mouth. Her pigtails are sharpened to delicate points by the water and she is looking about her, smiling. Her teeth are chattering with excitement.

My love for them flows through me so strong, so pure as I show them the game where we go underwater for as long as we can. I come up for air and move my hold so that for a moment they bob up like lifebuoys until I grasp each slippery neck and pull it back down under the surface.

I smile at their wide open eyes and round cheeks – it's almost like seeing double. They wriggle like larvae and I giggle with joy at how beautiful they are. Bubble-captions float up from them as they say goodbye and water flows into their mouths, ending drought.

I feel peaceful. I carry them to the bank of the dam and wrap them in their fresh, soft towels. I cradle them, rock them in the fading light, explaining that they'll always be safe now. I am singing them a lullaby when my husband finds us. At first he smiles to see us but when he understands (although he doesn't understand), he screams – a great roar that scares a flock of parrots into vivid green flight. I let him hold them and I comfort him as he looks at me with wild eyes.

*

I see him sometimes, when he comes to visit, all crumpled and quiet, missing his lost harvest. He always wears the same question on his weathered face but it's too complicated for me to understand. The voices bicker about who should answer it. They butt in before I can say anything, won't let me speak for myself.

So I just let them talk while I hold his hand. Then the nurses with needles shoo him away and spin me back into my long, dense nights and cocoon days. And when I dare, I glide and hover and dart, weightless, painless, free.

Farah Reza

Jesus, This is Heavy

Neither us of noticed it getting dark until it was night. The pub had filled with a group of men in pastel-coloured office shirts, talking and laughing too loudly for us to hear each other comfortably any more. I looked down at my drink, stirred it, and prepared myself.

'I'll call you if I can come,' she said. 'I'll see if it's okay with Jim.'

'Sure,' I said. 'Bring him if you like.' I hoped that my voice didn't sound weak or over-enthusiastic because I wasn't keen on the idea of Jim coming at all. I remember praying that he wouldn't come – the kind of praying that you do when you don't actually believe in God.

'I'll see what happens. He might have something on.'

I heard her perfectly well, but I pretended I hadn't. I wanted to see how she'd say it if she had to say it again, but it didn't sound any better. She almost shouted the words like I was stupid, her mouth forming large O's and her voice sounding like she was talking to a kid. Our eyes met and I could see dark splinters tremble against a lighter grey. Years ago, before we were friends, I had almost envied her for having eyes like that – the thick lashes made them look like some kind of rare flower. It was the closest thing to jealousy I had ever felt with her.

Emma squeezed her eyelids together as she scratched at something in the corner. I asked if she had something stuck in there, if she needed help, and there was a pause as she opened them wide and stared at the table. I was ready to give out some of the 'look up, look down' kind of advice that everyone knows.

'No,' she said. 'I think they're just sore from the radiators at work.'

'Can't you turn them down?' I creased up my forehead to look concerned. 'You don't want to be straining your eyes, especially when you're looking at a screen all day.'

She said, 'Yeah,' and her eyes narrowed before she looked away. She had been looking away like that all evening. Then there was silence that lasted a long time, and we looked at a man while he tripped and spilled his lager down his shirt.

'Do you want another?' I asked, pointing at her glass, though I knew we needed to think about making a move. I suppose I wanted to offer her something, to show her how much I was willing to give, but there's no easy way of saying that kind of thing.

'It's too late for another one, really,' she said. 'It's nearly eleven.'

I had what was left of my drink, whacked it down on the table and smiled at her. I thought that if I acted cheerful she might stop being so miserable. 'Finished,' I said. 'You done?'

She looked at me, her eyes moving across my face. 'Yeah,' she said, a softness creeping into her voice.

We were both a little drunk, but I wasn't going to ruin things by saying all the things that had been on my mind. Neither of us was drunk enough for that and it had been months since we talked properly about anything important. That was why I wanted her to come on Saturday. If I cooked her a meal and we opened a bottle of wine out in the garden, maybe we would start talking again.

I gave it one last try. 'Emma, if Jim can't come, will you still come?'

She thought about it, focussing on something on the other side of the room. Emma always looked like she was using up a lot of energy when she was thinking. She'd frown as she mulled things over.

'I'll try,' she said. 'I suppose he doesn't have to come. I just need to see if I can finish the spare room. The parents are in town next week.'

She smiled right at me, and I beamed back, but she still hadn't said she would come. She'd been sorting out that room for two weeks now, and there wasn't even much to sort out from what I had seen.

As she reached for her bag I got up and started to tuck my chair under the table. 'Jesus, this is heavy,' I said, because it really was a lot heavier than a chair should be. I had no idea what kind of wood could be that heavy. Emma got up, too, and didn't seem to have as much trouble with hers. She tucked it away without a word and put on her coat.

As we walked to the station together, we linked arms like we used to and she laughed at a joke I'd been saving. But later that night I just stared at the ceiling, and couldn't fall asleep until it was light.

Nina Robertson

Beanie Baby

The days are unexpectedly warm though the leaves are already turning. An Indian summer and a miracle that convinces her that everything can come good. Even he seems excited.

'We'll call him Bruiser, or Bonzo or Pele,' he says.

'It might be a her.'

'We'll call her... Bruisa!'

She imagines strollers and baby slings, cuddly toys and christenings and Christmases with toys piled under a tree. He isn't around a whole lot more, but he seems interested when she rings and describes the changes of her body. He buys her a teddy and smiles at other people's toddlers.

The cramps start pretty much immediately.

'They'll stop in time,' the doctor tells her, 'they're quite normal.'

She starts to enjoy the feeling of something alive inside her. Then the twinges stop. She can't find anything new to tell him about.

The night the cramps start again, she is waiting for him to ring. By the time she gets to the bathroom, pulls off her jeans and knickers and sits herself on the toilet, she is bleeding a scarlet flood, thick with black clots. She squats over the bowl, with her hands between her legs, straining the blood with her fingers to catch the baby when it comes. It lands hot in her palm, curled like a blind puppy and cold in an instant. She yelps, slumps down on the bowl, cradling her palm, the embryo, snug inside its mucousy bag. A silk purse, she thinks, a sow's ear. She sits and stares. She could flush it down the toilet like a dead goldfish.

She sits there – ten minutes, two hours? By the time she realises she is cold, her legs and belly covered in goosebumps, the sun is bleaching the bathroom walls. She pulls a length of toilet tissue from the roll and makes a nest of it on the edge of the bathtub and lays the baby in it. It could be a little bird, she thinks, all pink and featherless. Then she runs a bath. She takes off her remaining clothes, steps into the bath and watches the water turn scarlet as she sits down. She peers into the nest. Gently, with her fingers, she pulls back the membrane; it releases and wrinkles like cling film. The baby, about the size and shape of a kidney bean, lies exposed inside. She can make out the curve of the spine and the tiny protrusion of limbs. My beanie baby, she says, little Beanie.

'You can try again,' says her friend, Anna, who comes round as soon as she hears the news. She has bought flowers and chocolate.

'I don't think we will, though.'

There are heavy frosts. Matthew opens the freezer door. 'Jesus, Issy! What's this?' He takes a step back, staring into the icebox.

'I didn't know where to put her.' Issy is still in her dressing gown, sitting at the kitchen table sipping the tea Matthew has made for her. If she gets up and peers into the fridge with him, she will cry again, so she concentrates on her tea, her two hands cupped around it trying to warm herself.

'Right, well, we should bury it or something,' says Matthew as he slams the door shut.

'I don't have a garden. I don't have anywhere to bury her.'

'Well, bury it in the park or something. Issy, it's been months. You shouldn't still have it.'

'I can't bury her in the park.' She thinks of scuffed grass and litter-lined flowerbeds. 'I don't go to the park. How could I bury her in the park?'

'Well, decide on somewhere. You can't keep it here.'

Snow. Matthew is busy with work. He has to go to Belgium, Italy, France. Issy goes to work too and watches TV when she gets home. Anna takes her to the cinema, for a pizza, out shopping.

'Listen, Issy, I've got something to tell you. Phil and I have got engaged.'

'That's wonderful,' says Issy.

'Listen, Issy,' says Matthew on the phone, 'I've been offered a job in the States.'

'That's wonderful,' says Issy.

'You could always come and visit,' he says.

The days are getting longer. Issy takes the baby from the freezer, wraps it in a handkerchief and a plastic bag, and takes it to the wedding in her handbag. On the way she stops to pick up Matthew. He is waiting outside his flat with his suitcase. After the wedding, she will drive him to the airport. In the car they talk about the weather and Anna and her about-to-be-husband. At the registry office, they agree that Anna looks beautiful and that bride and groom both look really happy. After the reception, there is a disco. Issy sits and sips orange juice. She is waiting for a moment to slip out to the car and empty the contents of her handbag into Matthew's suitcase, but for now Matthew is beside her, perched on the edge of his seat watching the dancing.

'You two look like you need a top-up.' Phil has a champagne bottle in one hand and his other arm around Anna. The DJ is playing 'Love Train'. 'I hear you're off tonight, Matthew.'

'Yeah, that's right.'

'A job in the States?'

The dancers are forming a drunken conga.

'Yeah, it's an Internet start-up.'

'I thought they were over. They're all going bust now.' Phil tips the bottle over Matthew's glass.

'No, no. This one's got a really good product. It's going to definitely take off.'

'Well, this is finished, anyway.' Phil tips the bottle upside down. 'Come on, wifey, our guests are empty. We need more bubbly.'

Issy watches them heading towards the bar, arms around each other, giggling. She looks at Matthew. He is looking down at his empty glass, his shoulders slumped. He looks almost defeated, Issy thinks. She puts her hand gently on his back. The conga comes snaking past. Matthew puts down his drink, leaps to his feet and runs after it. He grabs on to the silver belt of the sequined dancer on the end and hangs on. For dear life, thinks Issy, watching him. He is awkward and out-of-step and completely familiar to her. The handbag sits perched on her knee. She can feel the weight of it. It is pink satin and beaded with glass.

On the way out into the hotel gardens, she takes a dessert spoon from the buffet and slips it into her jacket pocket. She crosses the lawn away from the building and the car park. There is a slight breeze. It carries the music from the disco; the insistent bass beat. It is already dark. She picks out the silhouette of a tree and heads towards it. It is a large, broad-branched oak and for a moment she leans against its trunk. When she starts to dig, the ground is hard and in need of rain.

Frances McCallum

Punctured

I t's a nice little street; narrow, as all such streets are, built for a time when the widest thing that needed to pass down the thoroughfare was a large family. It wasn't built for cars, especially not for big ones. There's a Victorian photograph of the street, taken around 1880, shortly after the houses were built – when it was a sort of housing estate, really. It looks impossibly wide. Mind you, the pavements are clear, the doors are closed and the only moveable object is a small girl in a white pinafore with a hoop. A hoop! She stares solemnly into the lens – a ghost from yesteryear. She could have stepped out of one of the houses. Or the photographer could have.

The residents have all lost wing mirrors over the years, and some people have simply given up on replacing them. They do a lot of craning and clawing at the back of the passenger seat when they're driving up and down their street. And partly because every now and then someone who isn't local drives down too fast, loses control and ricochets off one or more parked vehicles, no one has an expensive car. The other reason no one has an expensive car is that people on this street don't have a lot of money, and even if they did they wouldn't spend it on cars.

They're what someone who makes up catchy names for demographic groups might call Caring Creatives. They're teachers, potters, painters, nurses, midwives, writers, social workers, stonemasons. There's even an architect, but he's a bit embarrassed and is looking for a larger place out of the area, out of its proximity to the red-light district, the men in hoodies hanging out outside the corner shop. He'll still come back to buy his gear, although he probably won't pop in to say hello.

It's this proximity to the edgy part of town that makes living here exciting, because as well as the dealers and the prostitutes and the crackheads, there are also the pirate radio stations and the recording artists and the filmmakers. It's buzzing, but I don't think anyone behind those solid front doors would claim that it feels safe. That's not why you'd live here. It's also not the sort of place where everybody emerges from their houses at the same time and gets into their cars, like a *corps de ballet*, to drive to work. Things are more staggered, more haphazard.

When Steve, who actually has an office to get to, came out of number thirty-six one morning and saw that his tyres had been slashed on the side of the car parked on the pavement, he reacted with a weary, yet seething, resignation. He looked around as he fished his mobile out of his bag to phone work and report that he'd be a bit late. And he noticed that all the cars had slashed tyres. All the cars from about number fourteen to number fifty-eight had neat forty-five-degree slits about four inches long in the two tyres facing their owners' homes.

Next out was Anna from number thirty, who had to nip out before her partner went off to college. Her abandoned baby's screams followed her out of the door. She had to go to the art shop to collect a canvas they'd prepared for her – a brief moment of freedom. She nodded a smile at Steve who pointed at the tyres of her 2CV.

'You too, huh?' he said. 'Bastards.'

She looked down. 'Oh!' she said. 'God! Bastards.' And then she recovered and snapped back into her caring-socialist self. 'Poor things. They must have a rotten life to think that doing something like this is acceptable.'

'Yeah,' Steve muttered, 'probably.' And he looked at his tyres again. 'They're still bastards.'

Anna didn't feel she could argue.

'Well...,' he said, 'I'd better...' And, raising his arm, he ambled off.

There wasn't much Anna could do except call Trevor out. Despite her feminism, Anna still assumed that a man was genetically predisposed to be better at cars than she was. Even an academic. Trevor stood holding baby Charlotte, who was scarlet with screaming, and looked at the tyres with an expression that said very clearly: 'I'm a lecturer in eighteenth-century French literature, with a specialisation in philosophy. I don't know anything about tyres. Or childminding.'

Anna repeated her theory about the poverty of background of the perpetrator. Trevor was inclined to take Steve's line.

Rashid bundled out of his house, balancing a pile of books to be marked and simultaneously trying to lasso his own neck with yesterday's done-up tie. Anna and Trevor looked solemnly at him with that air of borderline smugness people have when they know something fractionally before you do. They pointed sadly at his car, leaning heavily on the pavement.

He followed their gaze. 'Oh, fucking hell! That's all I fucking need.'

Anna looked shocked and inclined her head at baby Charlotte, who didn't look shocked.

'Sorry,' said Rashid, 'but I mean... Fucking Hell! Sorry.' He stamped and growled. 'That's all I fucking need.' He went back indoors.

Rashid was a man who pulled a lot of sickies. He'd enjoy having a bona fide reason not to go in and teach the thick, aggressive yobbos who terrorised him and who were never going to learn Pythagoras' theorem in a month of Sundays, were he ever to give up so much time to them, which he'd be damned if he was.

There was no one else to tell. Anna suggested alerting people by ringing doorbells but Trevor pointed out that they might still be in bed, and perhaps waking people up in order to bring them bad news might not be taken in the spirit in which it was intended. They went back inside so that Trevor could clean the baby-sick off his jacket and get off for his ten o'clock lecture. Anna made a cup of tea and settled down to breast-feed with a copy of the *New Statesman*.

Vernon and Laura, the stonemasons, lumbered out of number forty-four and moved slowly, full of camomile and calm, towards the ancient car that doubled as their work van. They were renovating the stonework in a small chapel a few miles outside town and had been discussing over breakfast how they could feel the spirituality of the place suffusing their lives. Laura described how the souls of the satisfied dead were guiding her hand as she chipped away at the honey-hued Bath stone of the interior.

They got into their car and tried to pull away but realised from the tooth-tingling sound that something was amiss. Vernon stepped out and walked around the car twice before discovering the source of the problem.

They looked at each other, dumbfounded, and then they looked at the crowded street, realising that it was odd that no one should have left.

'It's not just us, Laura,' he said, which Laura thought was unusual, but then he had always had a slight persecution complex. Perhaps the dead invading his head were less satisfied than hers.

Luckily, they had her car parked a long way down the street. They'd think about it later.

The nurses in number fifty-two came out, wiping sleep from their eyes and talking about their appalling hangovers, and rode their bikes unsteadily past the lopsided cars, chatting about last night, not noticing a thing.

And then there was an air of calm about the place for a while. Cats sat on corner-posts and observed the stillness with satisfaction. The postman came and went. Baby Charlotte tried a half-hearted scream when she was put down for a nap. The slightly ragged plants in number fifty's window box shrugged off the night's moisture and uncurled slightly in the sunshine.

Tiny Ursula, the water colourist from number forty-two, whimsically named 'Rose Cottage', came out at about ten. She had recently involved herself in a physically and emotionally satisfying relationship at the age of sixty-two after ten years of happy, if solitary, divorce. She therefore passed these days in a haze of little sexual aftershocks, and memories of snippets of pleasurable conversation. She had picked all the plums from the tree in her garden and was taking a bucketful around to her daughter-in-law, who liked making jam.

Approaching her car, she saw what had happened. 'Maurice!' she called, rooted to the spot, 'Maurice!'

Maurice emerged from the house, toast crumbs clinging to his upper-lip moustache, slightly put out to have been forced to lay down the *Guardian* in the middle of a particularly interesting article about the nightclub scene in Newcastle.

Ursula was shaking her hands and quivering. His irritation faded as the opportunity for gallantry swelled before him.

'Look!' she whimpered. 'Look what someone's done! What am I going to do?'

He put his strong arms around her shoulders. 'You're going to pour yourself another cup of tea, Ursula,' he said, 'and you're going to look at the paper for a while and leave it to me.'

'Are you sure...?'

'It's not the first tyre I've had to change and I dare say it won't be the last.' His eyes twinkled with kindliness and affection. She thought, not for the first time, how nice it was to have a man about the house again.

So she went back inside and poured a nice cup of tea, settled down in the conservatory and tried to get over the shock, while Maurice went out with his jack, intent on sorting out at least one of the tyres. It felt good to be a protector. And it had been a long time.

Some time later, Anna, still attracted by the drama outside while having a second go at putting Charlotte down for a nap, rocked her way over to the window and froze. Looking down, she saw a hunched figure collapsed over a jack at the side of an elderly Renault 5. A thick ribbon of blackening blood ran round the edge of the car and pooled in the gutter. Setting Charlotte gently in the cot, she ran downstairs, out of the door and round to number fifty-four, where she pounded on the door. Bridget came to the door clad in a long kaftan over swinging breasts, her nappy-less toddler clinging to her skirts.

'There's been an accident. Someone's had a seizure...or something.' Anna pointed out of the door and they both looked at the foetal shape.

'Is he still alive?' asked Bridget, already detaching the child from her clothing.

'I don't know,' said Anna, suddenly aware that there was absolutely no way, ever, that she could touch a man who might possibly be dead. 'I didn't...'

'Dean!' called Bridget, and a tall, handsome, grizzled man with a roll-up in his mouth and a guitar in his hand appeared.

'Yes, love?'

She took an elastic band off her wrist and swept her greying hair back in a messy bun. 'Call the ambulance and take Lola?'

'Right, love.'

As Bridget and Anna headed off to the Renault 5, Dean peered out of the door.

Maurice had the jack clasped tightly in his two hands. It looked as though, at the moment his heart stopped, he had jerked upright and launched forward, hitting his head on the tarmac. Bridget listened to his heart and checked for vital signs.

Alistair came out of number forty-eight. Seeing the clump around the car, he went over. He bobbed around in and out of Bridget's light. 'God! What's happened? Bloody Hell! Have you seen the tyres?'

'Er, Alistair, would you mind...' Bridget looked up at him.

'Oh, sorry. I'll...er... make sure that no traffic comes along.' He took up a position a couple of yards from the action, arms outspread as if to catch oncoming cars. He was used to being a bit of a spare part, Alistair the nearly man, not really any good at anything, but very well-meaning. He worked for the local housing association, and was bent emotionally by the abuse meted out to him daily by angry clients. At least here no one would shout at him.

Bridget was getting to work. She was a midwife, really, more used to bringing life into the world than watching it slowly ebb away, but she'd been a nurse before. She could do this. She turned Maurice over and opened his shirt before placing her hand on his white-haired chest. She experienced a pang at the unaccustomed nearness of death, but suppressed it. She started to press rhythmically.

Anna squatted near her. 'Will he live?'

'I don't know.'

'Can I do anything?'

'No.'

Anna watched as Maurice's face drained of colour, the skin arranging itself loosely over the bones. 'Who is he?'

Bridget didn't stop. 'He's Ursula's partner. Moved in a couple of weeks ago.'

They both looked at the closed door of 'Rose Cottage'.

Rashid came out. 'Fuck.'

They ignored him.

'Little shits.'

Bridget looked enquiringly at him.

'Bastards that slashed all the tyres. Bet they didn't expect this.'

At that moment, a group of young lads sauntered up the street, hoods up, hands in pockets. They looked amused at the activity by the side of the car, but their amusement faded as they drew closer, close enough to see what form the activity had taken. Two boys looked at one another, jaws slack, eyes nervous.

Rashid looked up and his frustration with miscreant youth boiled over. He had no professional responsibility here. 'This your doing, lads, is it?'

'Rashid!' Anna hissed. 'You can't just assume...'

'Pleased with yourselves, are you, lads? Must have seemed like a bit of a lark, I suppose. Didn't think you might actually kill someone, did you? Didn't think you might actually fucking kill someone!' He didn't move towards them, not daring, not trusting himself, but also in habitual awe of a gang of confident seventeen-year-olds who sensed his fear.

'RASHID!' Bridget looked up. 'He's not dead yet. I have to be able to concentrate.'

'Didn't think someone might actually fucking DIE!'

'What you talkin' 'bout, man? Who you talkin' to, you wanker? You scum! Ain't nobody here killed nobody, you fuckin' wanker!' But they looked nervously at Bridget busy over the prone old man.

There was a whimper from the side. They all looked around to see tiny Ursula standing yards away. Alistair, Anna and Rashid moved as one to block her view. They hovered uncertainly, holding out their arms and waving slightly. No one knew what to say. Anna ran suddenly to put her hands on Ursula's fragile arms. But Ursula craned around on tiptoe, hooking her chin over Anna's shoulder and emitting an animal wail.

And just at that moment Bridget felt the body of Maurice deflate. Just like a tyre with the air let out.

Nick
Tucker

Waiting for Superman

The citizens of Metropolis are bored. We're close to throwing things at the walls we're so bored. Kettles and paint and suchlike. We don't care. That's how bored we are. There's nothing left to do. Nothing left to read about in the *Daily Planet*. Nothing. Husbands and wives bicker in the kitchens to enliven their days; children pinch their own legs and gangs of bored teenagers hurl themselves from our tallest buildings. Sometimes whole groups throw themselves off at once, from different buildings. Like synchronised swimmers toppling into a void, co-ordinating it all by mobile phone. But even then, even as they hurtle towards the ground, even then they still can't quite shake the great deadweight of boredom that's engulfed us all. Even as they plummet earthwards, they smoke their cigarettes and chat on their phones and wait idly for the red blur of Superman's cape to come streaking across the clear blue sky. Personally, we think he should let them splatter on the ground. Let them splosh. Just to teach them a lesson. But of course he can't. He has to save them. It's what he does. His dedication as unflappable as the cowlick on his forehead. But you have to wonder how Superman really feels, saving these kids. This can't be what he had in mind growing up in Smallville, struggling with those unearthly powers. But really, what can he do? He's saved the world. What else is left?

Nick Tucker

The Day We Just Flew

This was the day that me and Henry beat the world record for jumping so far it blows your mind. We just ran and jumped and oh boy we just took off. Our legs pedalling in the clear blue nothingness as we took to the sky. You should have seen us. Maybe you did. Maybe you were sitting in your garden that day, just minding your own business, when you looked up and saw two crazy, mind-blowing kids just take off, just fucking go. Maybe you were one of the people that left their houses and put on their running shoes to follow us on foot. Or maybe you put down your Sony PlayStation control-pad thing and got your dad to take you in the car and drive beneath those two crazy kids as they tore across the October sky, their legs pedalling and their arms flailing as dusk closed in and you were all like, Look at them fucking go. Jesus H. Christ. Have you ever seen anything like that? Man, that's insane, maybe they're not ever coming down. Was that you down there, in the blue hoodie pulled up over your head because your mum said that was the only way you were going out? You were just a tiny blue microdot to us, but we saw you. We saw everyone. We saw the long line of well-wishers snaking back across town. We saw the camera flashes go off, making everything look like phosphorus or glitter, like we were caught between the stars, speeding through the galaxy, our hearts doing crazy stuff in our chests as we wondered if we were ever coming down. We looked at each other and were like, Holy shit, what if this jump is too powerful? What if we've just broken all the known physical laws of the universe and we don't ever come down? What if we keep going and they have to send manned space flights up to hand us our dinner?

And maybe our mums will be really pissed off at having to prepare us special nutritional meals that NASA advised them to make, and what if they're sitting by the windows of the manned space flight looking angry as we kick our legs and flail our arms and are like, Sorry, it's just the jump was too good. We didn't realise our own strength. No one warned us we were this good. But then we hit it, the apex, and we knew, because for a moment we seemed to hang in the air, motionless, frozen in time, just looking down on the trees and rooftops and the crowds of people all staring up at us, too stunned to even cheer us on. Their minds just totally blown. But we knew; we knew we were coming down. We could feel the Earth sucking us back, could feel the tug of gravity in our chests, and we knew that the world record was smashed to smithereens and why hadn't we called up the Olympics and told them to get someone down to Henry's garden and judge our world record for themselves, because no one ever was going to get close to this again. No one in the history of jumping was ever going to jump like we were jumping now. But maybe they wouldn't have come anyway because our jump was just so amazing, so vast it would have obliterated all known records since back in the days of Greece in Athens and the Gods and stuff, and all of a sudden because of two twelve-year-old kids the Games would become like obsolete overnight because of us totally smashing the record books and they'd have to close down the Olympics and lose all that money in TV rights and stuff, and then there we were, coming down, hurtling towards the ground so fast like you wouldn't believe, like comets burning up in the sky and trailing space vapours, and we were scared shitless at the speed we were doing. And then we hit the ground and we went flying, rolling and spinning and tumbling the way racing cars do when they lose control and go careening across the chicane and into the barriers and totally explode, right into Henry's mum's flower patch where I totally thumped into him. But it didn't matter. It didn't matter a thing. Henry just jumped up and was like, Holy fuck, Bill, did you see that? Did you see us go? That must have been like eight, nine, maybe ten fucking feet. We goddamn cleared the fucking garden, almost. Oh man you shoulda seen us that day. We were on fire.

Jonathan Attrill

The Pike

'Pike-fishermen, like the pike itself, are a remarkable breed.'
Fauna Britannica

E| *sox lucius, otherwise known as the pike, is a fish unlike any other. It is common in the streams, rivers, lakes and even ponds of Great Britain, and yet it is a very uncommon fish in all other ways. Besides its scientific and everyday names, it is also referred to as the freshwater shark, water wolf, and lord of the stream. The reason for this is that, in its own realm, it is a fearsome and beautiful predator. Although the males of the species rarely grow beyond ten pounds in weight, females can grow much, much bigger than this. Thirty, forty, even up to seventy pounds. Their prey varies greatly, from the smallest minnows to birds and mammals.*

In appearance the pike is streamlined with an elongated face and a mouthful of razor-sharp teeth. The name itself derives from the Old English word for point. The sight of one of these fish torpedoing through the water, sunlight shimmering on its scaly back, is not one you'd soon forget. Believe me, I've seen it, although you'd have to spend many long hours waiting before you caught such a glimpse. The pike is a solitary creature, spending its time lurking in the depths until it senses prey. It has lived this way, virtually unchanged, for millions of years. It has an ancient, melancholy soul.

This comes from an article I once wrote on the pike.

My father loved pike. Today is Sunday, the day when I visit him.

'Afternoon, Pete,' the receptionist of the care home says cheerfully as I walk through the door.

'Afternoon, Julie.'

'A bit blustery out there, isn't it?'

'A bit. Where is he today?'

'He's in the sitting room. Snooker's on, I think. Just go through.'

In the large communal room I find him sitting, staring at the screen. Jimmy White is playing some newcomer I've never heard of. It's 3-1 to the newcomer.

'Hullo, dad,' I say, and sit in the empty chair beside him. He doesn't acknowledge me. Sometimes he does but today he doesn't; he just stares at the screen. Someone who didn't know him might think he was engrossed in the match, and once he would have been. He used to like the snooker, especially if Jimmy was playing, but not any more. He isn't seeing the television screen at all; he is far away in a world of his own making, perhaps of memory, perhaps of make-believe. No one really knows.

'Lena sends her love, dad.'

At last he hears me. 'Who?'

'Lena. My wife. You remember, you used to get on well with Lena.'

He frowns. 'Who are you any road?'

It's not a good day when he doesn't even recognise me, which is more and more often now. The illness is progressive.

'I'm Peter, your son.'

'Are you sure?'

'Yes, I should know.'

'Oh,' he says, 'I must have forgotten.'

'Never mind, it doesn't matter,' I say to comfort him, but it does. It does matter. It hurts when he doesn't even know I'm his son.

'The boys are well. Sam and Ben, your grandsons? They would have come today but they both had matches. I'll bring them next time.'

He isn't listening; he's looking at the screen again.

'I've brought you something,' I say, rummaging in my bag. 'Some grapes and some peaches. Do you want some?'

He looks at them as if they disgust him, then back at the telly. 'You're not my son. How could I have a son as old as you?' He gets like this; thinks he's still a young man. Sometimes, even now, he can talk about things from years back, when he first knew mum, as if they happened last week. But other things just seem to have vanished. I used to get frustrated with him, try and argue him into remembering certain things, but it just made him angrier and me even more upset. So now I back off, try and coax him, gently, to remember, hoping the right word in the right place might trigger something in his dying brain.

'Where's Mary?' he suddenly blurts out. 'Where's my wife?'

'She's just popped out for a minute, dad,' I say. I don't tell him she won't ever be coming back. 'I'll just leave the fruit in the bag for now. It's on the table.'

After a few minutes I say, 'Do you remember when we caught Mona?'

He turns his head, doesn't look at me but into space, with a slight frown as if he's staring into a mist, looking for something he knows is there but can't quite see. 'I don't know,' he says quietly.

'You must remember Mona.'

There was a small lake in the woods behind the village we lived in back then, before the pit closed down and we had to move away. Somewhere in that lake was a massive pike. We called her Mona after Willy Grimshaw's wife, because she was called Lisa, had a face like a fish, and was constantly moaning at Willy, who worked down the mine with dad.

Some people thought it was Bob Wilkins caught Mona. Apparently he walked into the Lion's Head one Sunday morning with this bloody great fish and told everyone he'd caught her at last. They had it mounted and hung behind the bar. It was a big one all right, and no one doubted it really was Mona. Except dad. He walked in there one day and looked up at that fish on the wall and said, 'That isn't Mona. Isn't big enough.'

'What you talking about?' Bob said to him, riled. 'It's twenty-three pounds that. Been weighed proper. Official like.'

'Well it might have been, Bob, but that isn't Mona. Mona's thirty pounds at least.'

'You're just jealous, Joe. You been after Mona for years, but it were me that caught her.'

Dad just stood there looking up at that fish on the wall, shaking his head. 'No,' he said, as if to himself, 'that isn't Mona.'

Then he turned to me and said, 'Right then son, we'll have a quick one and get back for lunch.' He bought himself a pint and me an orange juice, and we sat outside together in the sun. We didn't talk much that day, or any other day really; he wasn't a big talker my dad. But I could tell he had something particular on his mind.

Then, as he neared the end of his pint, he said to me, 'How do you fancy going fishing with me, Peter?'

'Yeah, great,' I said. I'd never been that interested in fishing before but hearing about this fish had changed all that. Suddenly it was like my dad had become some kind of Captain Ahab, and Mona was this mythic creature. I loved stories and I'd read an abridged version of Herman Melville's tale earlier that year. I didn't really know what it was all about at that age, but I knew it was a great story. And now I would have a chance to be in a version of it myself.

'Then sup up lad, and we'll get some of your mother's lunch and go out today.'

That afternoon, after lunch, he took me into the yard with him, opened up the shed where he kept his fishing gear, and started searching for whatever items it was he was looking for, handing strange things back to me as he found them. First was his own rod. I knew it because I'd often seen him go off down the road with it on his shoulder. Then he found another. 'This'll do,' he said, handing the rod to me. 'There, that's yours now.'

'But I don't know what to do with it.'

'Don't worry about that. I'll show you. Just look after it.'

When he'd gathered together everything he felt we needed, he put it all in a large bag and we set off for the lake. It was a lovely midsummer's afternoon and we took the short cut across Clither's Meadow. The heat glared down on us but he walked with his head up, squinting into the sun. He loved the sun.

I never went down a mine; he didn't want me to. Lots of the lads I went to school with followed their fathers down the pit, but not me. Once I asked him what it was like down there. 'It's like being buried alive,' he said. When I was about six or seven there was an accident and he was trapped underground for a whole day. Mum was hysterical, convinced he was going to die down there. Eventually they got them out again, but he said to me as my mother clasped him to her with tears running down her face, 'Whatever you do, son, don't do no job where you can't see the sky.' His face was black as the face that used to be on Hartley's Jam, and when they parted mother's pale-blue dress was filthy.

When we got to the lake that day I followed him halfway round before he finally found a spot he liked and said, 'This looks alright.' He started to unload the things I'd seen him pack before we left: line, traces, hooks, and all kinds of other stuff. 'I'll show you what to do today, son, you just watch. Gradually you'll get the hang of it all and be able to do it yourself.'

I watched as he set up the two rods, astounded at his expertise, the way he knew exactly what to do. Now and again he would tell me what a certain piece of tackle was for, but not too much; he didn't want to overload me with information on the first trip. At one point he opened a small plastic box, revealing an array of strange, feathery creatures. 'Now these,' he said, 'are the flies. What we're doing is called fly-fishing, see?'

'What they for?'

'These little things are our bait. They're what's going to lure her in. Pick yourself one out.' They were all different colours, some even had eyes. It was almost as if they had different personalities. Seeing that I couldn't decide, he reached in and pulled one out for me. 'This one's a good one, have that.'

'Do you think we'll get her today, dad?' I asked as he fitted the fly to my rod.

'Maybe, but I wouldn't put money on it. Fishermen round here have been after old Mona for years. The great thing about fishing, son, is that it teaches you patience. That, and the fact you're always out in open air where you can breathe proper and feel the sun or the rain on your skin.'

A burst of applause comes from the telly. Jimmy White has just completed a hundred break. 'I can't remember, I can't remember,' dad says, starting to get agitated.

'Don't worry, dad, don't worry. It's all right, it's not that important.' In a way it's reassuring for me, his agitation. It's like when he was first getting ill a long time ago and he'd know he had lost something but couldn't remember what. He would get frustrated and angry with himself. So I knew whenever he got like that something was close enough for him to know he'd lost it.

It's selfish of me to feel relieved when he's upset in this way, but I can't help it. Then again, it's selfish of me to have put him in this place anyway. We tried having him home with us after mum died, but it was just too much. Before that we'd been trying to convince mum she couldn't cope, but she wouldn't listen. Then when she went, and it came down to it, I couldn't put him in a home myself. Not at first. But the stress of looking after him – well, it was too much even for us. It was putting a strain on our marriage, and the kids were upset all the time. It wasn't the physical strain of looking after him; it was emotional. Seeing him like that hour after hour, day after day, I just couldn't cope.

And now here he is, and here I am visiting on another wet Selby Sunday afternoon.

'Do you fancy going out, dad?' I ask him.

He looks at me as if I'm mad or something. 'It's pissing down out there.'

'Yes, I know.' I smile. 'We could take an umbrella. Have a walk round the garden.' They've got a nice garden here.

'If you like, then.'

I help him put his coat on and ask Rita, the head nurse, if it's all right; we won't be long. She says of course in her strong West Indian accent, and tells dad his son is a nice man. He looks at her blankly then nods in passive agreement.

Outside is a little patio and beyond that a lawn. There's a pond near the back wall with goldfish in it. I lead him over to it, the umbrella arcing over both our heads.

'Do you work here or summat?' he asks.

'No,' I reply, 'I'm just a visitor.'

'What do you do with yourself the rest of the time?'

'I'm an editor for an angling magazine. Fishing.'

'I know what angling means.'

The raindrops are pelting the surface of the little pond.

It was raining the day we caught Mona. A year had gone by and I'd become a real fisherman by then, although I still had a lot to learn. You never stop learning the art of fishing. Week after week we'd been out on that lake in all kinds of weather, sitting together, often in silence. We'd caught a fair few by then, including some pike – I caught a twelve-pounder myself once. But never a sight of Mona.

That summer, dad got an idea. He bought a little rowing boat. Once it had been blue but by the time we got it most of the paint had gone. It was barely big enough to seat the two of us but we just about managed. We would moor it out of sight in some reeds at the edge of the lake and, just in case anyone else did find it, dad painted *Property of Horton and Son* on the side.

It was raining that late-summer day as we rowed out onto the lake. I remember dad saying to me, 'I got a funny feeling today, lad. Like summat special's going to happen.'

We must have sat there in the middle of the lake for three, four hours that afternoon. Nothing. It seemed the fish just weren't in the mood. I'd suggested packing up a couple of times, but dad said, 'Give it a bit longer'.

The rain had stopped and there was a break in the clouds and the water shone a kind of silver like I'd never seen before. And that's when it happened. I felt a tug on my line different to anything I'd felt before out there. 'I've got something,' I said.

'Well, start reeling, son, start reeling.'

I started turning the reel but almost immediately there was this terrific resistance. 'I can't, it's too hard.'

'Quick, give it to me, son,' he said, taking the rod from me. 'It's a big one, alright.' He started reeling it in. Even he was struggling (and he was a fair-sized man in those days) and the boat was rocking. I held on to the boat's sides and stared at the water where the line dipped below the surface. It seemed to take an age and I thought it would never come up, but all the time he was reeling in the wire on the rod, which seemed about to break.

And then she broke the water's surface in a spray of silver sparks, the most magnificent fish I'd ever seen. I've seen bigger, a lot bigger, in the years since, but never anything so beautiful. And I've never experienced anything like I did in that moment. The struggling fish gleamed a brilliant green and a kind of gold on its underside. I heard dad breathe in awe. 'Look at the size of that.'

'Is it her, dad? Is it Mona?'

'Aye, lad, it's her alright.' He pulled her into the boat and laid her in the net between us, wriggling and flapping her tail.

'That'll show Bob Wilkins, eh dad?'

'I'm not bothered about Bob Wilkins,' he said. 'He'll never believe us any road.'

'But he'll have to, they'll all have to, when we take her back.'

'We're not taking her back.'

I didn't understand. For over a year I'd had visions of us striding through the streets of the village with Mona slung over dad's back. Marching right into the Lion's Head and saying, 'Right, you can take that old thing down. This is the real Mona.'

'What do you mean?' I asked. 'I thought we'd mount her in the pub.' I knew we usually threw them back, unless we fancied fish for tea; but this was different. This was Mona.

'We're putting her back as soon as I've got this hook out of her mouth, son. It's not right to keep a creature like this out of water for long. And you should only kill summat if you're going to eat it or wear it, and I'm not about to eat Mona. Besides,' he said, looking down at the fish, 'a beautiful thing like this belongs where it belongs.'

He reached down and, with expert fingers, unhooked her. I helped him lift her up and we threw her over the side into the water to disappear forever.

I learnt more that day than any other day in my life.

The rain is harder now, pinging off the umbrella I'm holding for both of us as we gaze at the goldfish in the little pond.

'I used to fish, I think,' he says.

'That's right, you did. You were a good fisherman. The best.'

'Was I?' he asks, with a glimmer of pride in his face.

'Yes, you were.'

'What did I catch again?'

'Pike.'

'Pike,' he says slowly, as if it's the most wonderful sound in the world.

In a few minutes I'll take him back inside for his tea.

Justine Mann

The Visit

Sitting in the darkness, you're wondering how it came upon you so quickly. It seems only days since you looked at the calendar, reassured it was a comfortable distance. You nurse a mug of tea against your cheek, though the remnants turned cold an hour ago.

On the kitchen table lies the card, still blank. Though you ponder, you will write the same words as always. Later, they will read it to her in their sugary tones and in a week or two, faded from the sun, it will be taken from the windowsill and placed with the others in a box beneath the bed.

The pipes gurgle into life and, as if this were a cue, you slowly rise from the table. Upstairs, Malcolm is still sleeping, his face half-buried into your vacant pillow. You take care to tiptoe across the creaking boards as you gather your clothes. The shower is barely warm but you stand oblivious beneath the spray, blinking into its downpour.

The drive is a grey concrete monotony. The sky leaden, each cloud packed tightly with rain. A hundred miles, then fifty, then ten. Finally, the familiar driveway crunches beneath the wheels. Through the windows, you see the dark shadows of the residents moving within. Guilt is already prickling your neck. For a moment you pause, gripping the steering wheel and watching the reflection of clouds skimming over the upstairs windows. As you climb the steps to the entrance, you feel your chest tighten.

The receptionist is wearing tinsel in her hair. She smiles warmly. 'Merry Christmas, Sarah.'

You're wondering how they remember you between visits.

'Good journey?'

'Thanks.'

'Your mum's still in her room. If you could just sign in.'

As you place the flowers on the counter and take hold of the pen, your hands are shaking.

Despite the early hour, the corridor is in semi-darkness. To your right, the lounge is half full, a game of cards in progress at one table. The television screeches out to its audience: a solitary man hunched forward in the front row straining to hear. A staff member leads a woman slowly down the hall, her stooping frame dressed elaborately for an outing. She mutters as you pass, drawn-on eyebrows arching.

And then you reach your mother's room: number six. The door is open slightly but you knock anyway.

'Sarah, it's lovely to see you. Look, Edith, Sarah's come to see you.'

Your eyes skim the room impatiently and settle on your mother. She sits propped up in the armchair. Her face more shrunken than you remember. Her posture somehow awkward, as if she's been posed like a doll for your entrance.

She turns her face towards you. But there is no spark. No ignition. You knew to expect it, but it unnerves you still. 'She's lost weight again.'

'Some, yes. She's been really looking forward to your visit.'

'Yes, I can see that.'

The woman fires a sharp glance over her glasses before continuing to coax your mother to take the pills from a small plastic cup. She is looking into the woman's face like a child, trusting but unyielding until the last possible moment. She gulps at the water, eyes flickering to the ceiling. You gaze with alarm at the quantity and dimensions of the pills. There is a rainbow of brightly coloured capsules. Others, of an impossible size and shaped like mini torpedoes, sit in a separate beaker.

The woman spots your expression and chuckles. 'Don't worry, dear, she won't be swallowing those. Please excuse us.'

And for a moment, as the bathroom door closes behind them, you are troubled by the jealousy rising within you.

Without her presence, the room is soulless, her few favourite ornaments marooned in its bland uniformity. Your grandmother's silver hairbrush and mirror sit awkwardly on the white chest of drawers. A rebellious flash of purple across the bed: the dressing gown you gave her last Christmas. You lift it towards you and feel the remaining warmth. Then you replace it gently and take the flowers from their wrapper.

It was a Mother's Day when you proudly presented your first gift: a bunch of daffodils wrapped in pink paper. There were tears in her eyes as she admired them. She hugged you tightly, and you watched proudly as she arranged them in the china vase, stroking each flower with her hand and inhaling an imaginary perfume.

That same Sunday, she taught you to make your grandmother's chocolate cake. She slid it into the oven and warned you fiercely not to open the door. Instead, you guarded it anxiously through the glass. To distract you, she took down the old family album. And as you flicked through its worn pages, she retold familiar stories, always revealing extra details for you to savour.

They emerge from the bathroom. 'There we are – all done.' The woman beams and your mother returns the smile shyly. 'Let me put those beautiful flowers in water.' Then much louder. 'Edith, look at the beautiful flowers Sarah has brought you.' The woman stands before the bouquet and draws in an exaggerated breath, nostrils flaring. Your mother stares back blankly, looking at each of you in turn.

The woman gives you a conspiratorial wink as she sweeps out of the door. 'What woman could ever resist flowers, eh? You'll stay for the carols and mince pies, Sarah?'

You turn to take off your coat and in the awkward silence fold it several times over, carefully brushing away some imaginary fluff. 'Mum? How are you?'

She mimics your smile but her eyes remain unlit. Her mouth oozing. Her tights are twisted round her legs all the way down to her slippers. They let her sit there all day, those twists rubbing against her skin.

'Where's Ruth?'

Your chest tightens again. Your voice is gentle, but firm. 'Ruth's gone, mum.'

Like a child she repeats after you, as if speaking new words without comprehending their meaning: 'Ruth's gone. Gone.'

You picture your garden, the tree she helped plant there. You had knelt, tenderly pressing at the earth, an unceasing weight inside drawing you downwards.

'She'll always be your child, no matter how tiny she was, no matter how short her life. You must never forget that, Sarah. You must come here when you're feeling it. Come here and talk to her.'

You stand up from the bed and turn to face the window. 'Let me take you for a walk. Are you feeling up to a walk? I'll see if they'll let me take you for a walk.'

Outside, the grounds are filling with families. Grandchildren and great-grandchildren spilling from cars. The Sunday before Christmas. One last chore before they can enjoy the holiday, consciences clear. She is distracted. You fill the space with chatter. Malcolm has been promoted. You are visiting France again this summer. The garden is looking lovely. Aunty Sheila sends her love.

Her steps are slow and her breathing laboured. You are leading; she is following. You steer her towards a bench and watch her sit slowly and carefully. There is a little diluted wintry sun now, warming your faces. You take her hand and close your eyes. It feels smaller and thinner, as if she is slowly disintegrating.

'Daddy'll be home a little later.' It comes without warning. 'He's won on the horses again, gone off for a little celebration.'

You hesitate at first. This is what you've been dreading most. As your eyes adjust to the light again, however, you see hers shining brightly for the first time. It reminds you of a Christmas morning years ago. Malcolm and your father had gone to fetch some coal from the shed. You were both preparing lunch in the kitchen. And when she handed you a sherry, you declined and whispered an explanation into her ear, rubbing your palm over the growing expanse of belly beneath your shirt. Her eyes had brimmed with happiness for the rest of the day.

You begin quickly, eager not to break the spell, as if remembering lines in a play. 'Will he let me have a dog, mummy?'

'Ooh goodness, Sarah, a dog!'

'Well, a cat then.'

'Maybe a rabbit, sweetheart, or a guinea pig? A cat can be so unfriendly.'

'Can I have it on my bed?'

'Your bed! I'm not sure what your daddy would have to say about that now.'

She is laughing. But then your phone rings: Malcolm. And in the time you scramble to turn it off, the smile has gone again and in its place the now familiar haunted look, a mixture of confusion and fear.

Back in her room, you fluster from wardrobe to drawer, to table, checking clothing, food supplies, papers. You stare at the smooth blue circle of soap nestling on her sink, at the bristles of her toothbrush slightly worn. 'Is there anything you need, mum?'

There is only silence.

'Do you promise me you'll eat something? Will you eat something with me now?'

You turn your back and tell yourself to stay calm. You will soon be home again. Malcolm will open the front door when he hears your car on the drive. He will read your face and hold you for as long as it takes. 'Bring her back if you want to. If it makes you happy.'

There is a boys' choir in the sitting room. The lights twinkle on the tree and the gas fire is turned up high. Two of the boys are giggling nervously at the array of strange faces before them. Another, at the back, farts loudly and the entire group dissolves into laughter. You can't help smiling and feeling a little envious of their innocent fun.

When finally they sing it sounds eerie. These fledgling, youthful voices filling a room stifled with decay. The choirmaster is strict and over-animated. The boys are momentarily angelic, their mouths exaggerating the shapes of words. Between each carol the audience claps enthusiastically and at the end the boys gladly tuck into the mince pies.

And then it's time to leave. Though you hate to come, this is really the worst moment. You become upset and then she is frightened. You clasp her hand and rub her translucent skin back and forth too quickly. And then you count to three and walk away without turning back.

You drive too fast. There are tears stinging your eyes and the radio is blaring. At the motorway services, you avoid the crowds and walk up to the glass bridge with your coffee to watch the cars whizz beneath. You dial your sister's number. You desperately want to talk to her but find yourself telling her voicemail in a shaky voice that your mother is the same. Nothing to report.

Malcolm sits you in the kitchen with a glass of red wine while he sets about frying the fish. The newspaper is spread out before him on the table, muddy garden boots discarded. You drink in each comforting detail, longing to erase the day. When you speak, the conversation meanders in a familiar way. Malcolm pauses occasionally and watches you intently. He doesn't need to speak; his eyes tell you all. But this time you acknowledge he is right. Later that month, you will dig up the earth and plant another tree next to Ruth's.

Patricia Debney

After Last Night's Rain

The children run out like pondskaters across the grass, zig-zagging, their toes hardly touching. They spin, weave between what look like glossy button mushrooms sprung up overnight, a scene from *Fantasia*. They bring everything to life, leave trails in the settled dew like fairy dust.

Nothing lasts forever. By midday they are hot and tired, and we venture out, expecting casualties, expecting the creamy pieces littering the lawn. In the shade of a tree we come upon one: not a mushroom, plump chunks still good to eat, but a snail, its white splintered shell still wet with juices, disconnected, its body turned as though kicked, aside. And all around it, like spokes in a wheel, the others gather, stretching out their blind fingers in curiosity or sympathy.

Sally Hinchcliffe

Witching Hour

[S]omewhere in the spiritual, if not the geographical, heart of Middle England there is a small, honey-hued town whose name is not, although it ought to be, Market Burden. Nestled in a crook of the great grey Thames, in wet winters almost engulfed in its greasy embrace, it has a market cross, a high street, a war memorial, two churches, and a town council. This, like the Scouts, the judo club, the WI and the Market Burden film society, meets in the one community hall. It is possible that there would be more going on in Market Burden were there either more community halls or more days of the week. The council's day was Thursday. Its chair was Harold.

Harold was the sort of man who could get from nought to incandescent in sixty seconds. Given any sort of subject, faced with a definite opinion not his own and from a standing start, he could be in an eye-popping rage of opposition before the thought had even been fully expressed. His wife had secured for herself a peaceful evening once a week by gently pointing out one morning over breakfast that he'd be mad to put himself forward for a position on the council. Harold had in the last six council meetings variously opposed nuclear power, the Euro, the Internet, a new bus shelter, cutting the bus service, public transport in general, and a bench opposite the war memorial. He sat at the head of the council table in a three-piece tweed suit, polished brogues and a lather of indignation. He had a round face and retreating hair, and had looked in his forties all his life. Now that he was moving into his fifties, it was as though he were going back in time. His plumpening cheeks and shinily emerging scalp reminded Janet Morris of nothing so much as a cross baby.

Janet was a woman who practised reasonableness as an art form. She had the slinky even-handedness of the professional facilitator, someone who, in defiance of all geometry, could see both sides of every question, and come up with a third that squared the circle. She could hear what people were saying, and understand where they were coming from. When she worked in insurance she could leave a house with everyone in it feeling that, finally, here was someone who really sympathised with their position, and what on earth were they supposed to do with this policy they'd just taken out? She had desperately wanted to chair the council but the others had been swayed by the force of Harold's rage at the prospect of having either a chairwoman, or worse, a madam chairman, so she had settled for being the power behind the throne. She steered the winds of his fury, she made suggestions that sounded like questions and demurrals that sounded like support, and tacked and ducked and swung and retreated until she seemed to bow to defeat, and slid out of the room with the decision she had wanted all along.

Besides Janet and Harold, there were four other council members. The details of three of them – the woman who kept dogs; the woman who didn't like dogs; and the farmer whose main crop was subsidies – you can fill in for yourselves. They only spoke when their subjects of special interest came up. The final member sat at the end of the table, slouched in his chair with his feet already pointing out the door. One hand was in his trouser pocket in a way Janet found disturbing. The other toyed with a pencil in a way even the woman who kept dogs found disturbing. Daniel Mavis was younger than anyone else in the room by a good fifteen years. He had loped into the small market town three years before, appearing to possess only the clothes he stood up in. He had taken the job of assistant groundsman for the big house that stood at the edge of the town, and when the old groundsman retired and was forcibly evicted from his tied cottage and re-housed on a sink estate in Morseby, Daniel got his job and his house. And he also got his seat on the council; the groundsman of Burden house had always sat on the council and just because there seemed to be something fishy about the way the whole thing had come about, that didn't mean you could break with tradition. He sat at the end of the table and slouched, and wore an earring and the same old jumper he'd walked into town in, and seemed to find the proceedings amusing. He had dark hair and sleepy green eyes and poor hygiene and whenever they saw him all of the women in the town found themselves thinking how disgusting it would be to go to bed with him and they wouldn't be able to get that thought out of their minds until they'd fought with their husbands over nothing and lain up all night crying and wondering what might have happened had things turned out differently.

The day after he got the job and the cottage and the seat on the council, Janet had come round to show there were no hard feelings, and to try to recruit him as an ally in her war against Harold. Daniel was dividing clumps of daisies with a spade, driving the blade down hard through their tangled roots. He stopped when she came by. She stuck her hand out and he looked at it for a while, before wiping his own on the seat of his trousers and taking it. His was cool and still in hers, and he looked at her in a way that made her wonder if he was secretly and hopelessly in love with her. She felt sorry for him, pining silently for an older woman who had kept her figure and still dressed quite stylishly despite the lack of decent shops in the town. She held his hand for a beat longer than was necessary, and made a point afterwards of always stopping for a chat when she saw him so that he could see she was really quite ordinary and too old for him, making sure she mentioned her husband frequently. That way she hoped to wean him off this hopeless crush so he could find a more suitable woman, someone his own age. The groundsman's cottage was a little out of her way on her route into town but she took the detour gladly, just for those mornings when she would see him emerging, stretching and rumpling his disorderly hair, pulling on his jumper sometimes, exposing an inch or so of hairy, lean belly. Then she could wave, matter-of-factly, giving a cheery and indifferent greeting. After she saw the pale, frail redhead emerging with him one morning, wearing his shirt, however, she went back to taking the direct route. That redhead broke a lot of hearts in Market Burden.

After minutes of the last meeting, which were approved, and matters arising, of which there were none, the next item on the agenda was Market Burden's annual bonfire night. Janet guided the discussion as smoothly as ever. She started by suggesting that it might be held early, to coincide with Halloween. 'It seems to be very popular with the kids these days.'

'Halloween?' Harold muttered, warming up, 'load of American nonsense.

Halloween – might as well start celebrating Thanksgiving. Why don't we all put on tall hats and buckled shoes and thank the Indians for showing us how to grow corn? Hordes of children pouring round the village dressed as ghosts, too lazy to make a proper costume, just a couple of eyeholes cut out of a sheet, demanding money with menaces. Oh, you young people might not remember,' he went on, addressing his remarks now to Daniel whom he thought deserved a good horsewhipping and who was directing his eyes at the ceiling, 'but back when I was a lad we had to make a real effort on Halloween, none of these shop-bought costumes, sing a song or recite a poem and after all that, you'd be lucky if you got an apple or a boiled sweet for your efforts. Halloween. Pah! Fifth of November, that's the date for bonfire night.'

Having got the date she wanted, Janet moved on to the budget.

'Budget? What do you need a budget for? Bonfire's a bonfire, pile of dead wood; there's enough of that lying around in the streets as far as I can see. Litter, skips full of perfectly good things, furniture that people throw out, more money than sense these days.'

The farmer murmured something about fireworks, although Janet knew this was a mistake. They'd had no fireworks the previous year because, Harold had said, they made too much noise, and children were letting them off in the street, no lighting the blue touch paper and retiring like they had in his day. Oh no, they were just throwing bangers everywhere with no respect. Last year's bonfire night had been a miserable failure and half the town had slunk off to see the fireworks run by the cricket club in Moresby instead.

Janet said diffidently, 'Of course, fireworks do frighten the dogs.'

'Oh, we can't have that,' piped up the woman who kept dogs, 'my Trixie and Popeye are terrified by fireworks; they can barely sleep for weeks afterwards. I had to take Trixie to the vet, have her put on tranquilisers, last time.'

The notion of a dog on tranquilisers – 'Can't you just take her out for a good walk, get her to pull herself together, woman?' – was enough to have the fireworks' budget doubled. Janet pulled her papers together with the satisfaction of a job well done and prepared to arrange the date for the next meeting. But Harold was a stickler for the agenda, couldn't bear things done sloppily, might as well do them properly or not at all. 'Now, any other business?'

There was a stir from the end of the room. Daniel uncoiled his feet from the chair legs, pulled his hand from his pocket, cleared his throat. 'I propose we turn off all the street lights in the town and have one night of complete darkness.'

'Good lord,' said Harold. 'In God's name, why?'

'Why not?' asked Daniel.

Harold's mouth opened and shut silently, and his eyes flicked round the room. He could think of a dozen reasons why not, but all of them came across as opinions and so he felt obliged to oppose them. Janet, still smarting about the redhead, spoke without thinking, something she hadn't done since 1987. 'It would be dangerous.'

'Dangerous?' cried Harold. 'Good God, woman, we're practically in the country here, skies ought to be dark at night, dammit. Why, back in the war, there was a total blackout every night – nobody died.' Everyone nodded, although only the woman who didn't like dogs was actually old enough to remember the war, and she'd been terrified by the blackout. 'Why, I remember as a boy seeing the stars every night. Kids these days don't even know what stars are, think the Milky Way is a chocolate bar. Rotting their teeth with chocolate all the time, when they should be out there learning about the stars.'

Startled by this sudden expression of a positive opinion from their chair, the council approved the motion unanimously. The night of the next full moon, for one hour at midnight, all of the lights would be turned off. Even Janet acceded, convinced there would be some legal reason why they couldn't actually do it. The date of the next meeting was agreed in record time and they all trooped out into the orange semi-murk they had learned to call the dark.

Market Burden council had very few powers besides bus shelters and bonfires, but it turned out that street lighting was one of them. There was a brief outcry in the local paper against the scheme, which caught the attention of the national press, and Janet found herself interviewed on local radio, between a wind-farm debate and a report about the sighting of a mysterious giant rabbit. As spokesperson for the council, she championed the blackout strongly, setting aside her own personal feelings. Hearing the broadcast later, she found herself convinced by her own arguments.

After that, there was no stopping it. The vicar and the priest set aside theological differences and agreed to switch off the floodlights on their churches. The war memorial society agreed to turn off the lights on the war memorial. The highways agency consulted their lawyers, and the legislation, and could find nothing forbidding the switching off of street lights in peri-urban areas. A question was asked in the House of Lords, but nobody answered it. The local bed and breakfast reported an upsurge in enquiries from astronomers. One cult in California claimed it was a sign from God, and another denounced it as the work of the Devil, and both put so many links from their websites to Market Burden council's that it briefly became the top-rated site on the Internet and won a national award. Harold accepted it graciously on behalf of the council and became something of a cult figure in knowing London circles. That season, polished brogues and tweed suits featured prominently on the catwalks in Milan, but that would probably have happened anyway.

On the first night of the full moon, at five minutes to midnight, Harold, Janet and Daniel, accompanied by a local news film crew, walked slowly from the centre of the town, setting the blackout in motion. First the war memorial and the market cross blinked out and disappeared. Then the two churches. The light on the spire of St Mary's was on a separate switch and it briefly floated, disembodied, above the town before it too disappeared. The little procession moved out towards the edge of the town and as they went, junction box by junction box, the darkness devoured the street lights. The woman who kept dogs stood at her front window and watched the blotting out of the town. A strange, throaty, vibrating noise made her look down. Trixie was growling. Every vestigial wolf gene in her tiny body was awakened and she was snarling and hackled with rage. As the three figures passed the house, the low, menacing rumble rose until Trixie's whole body was consumed by it and the woman who kept dogs took an involuntary step backwards.

Finally, the owner of Burden House found himself obeying the nod of his own groundsman towards the switch of the external security light, and the last light in the town vanished. The town had been deemed to extend only as far as the two speed-limit signs that stood next to the 'Welcome to Market Burden' board. As a concession to road safety, these were to remain illuminated – Janet noticed that someone had added 'Twinned with Hades' in a gothic script under the town name. Beyond, there was nothing but darkness. The woman who kept dogs looked at the window again but this time all she could see was the reflection of her own face, white and staring. Trixie had subsided. She closed the curtains.

Janet contemplated their handiwork. They were standing on a slight rise, looking down over a bowl of darkness. To her right, she could hear Harold's slightly laboured breathing. To her left, she sensed the contained stillness of Daniel. She felt a shared sense of purpose with him, a connectedness, a feeling of achievement. He was so close they were almost touching.

One by one, people from the town emerged, blinking, into the darkness. The moon tore through the last shreds of cloud and the whole town was washed with its light. People stood on the streets, misnaming constellations, and pointing out Venus in every direction. Doors stood open, neighbours talked to each other, and children ran unhindered through the street. The camera crew tried to film but a crowd formed around their lighting rig, muttering, until they turned it off. On every horizon the dull orange glow of other towns could be seen, eating into the night sky, but above Market Burden there was only a sparkling band of stars. The Milky Way.

Janet, buoyed, reached out both hands to link arms with the men on either side of her. Her right gathered a substantial armful of tweed and warmth. Her left scooped empty air. Daniel had gone, and Janet and Harold walked back into the town together, suddenly grateful for any human contact.

The next morning the groundsman's cottage was dark and empty. It was a couple of weeks before the full amount of what had been stolen from Burden House was realised. There was a rash of reports of two-headed goats being born in the area, and a boom in mysterious, dark-headed, sleepy-eyed babies, but that was put down to hysteria. The news footage, when examined carefully by the team from *Crimewatch*, was found to have no usable images of Daniel. He appeared only as a shadowy figure at the edge of a few shots. Market Burden retreated back into well-lighted obscurity, and the council was merged into a unitary authority. Janet and Harold had an affair. Everyone managed with some effort to forget the night of darkness at witching hour, except for the children and for Trixie, who came out and shivered and howled, every month, at the full moon.

Ella
Saltmarshe

Accession

'We are bringing into the EU family 10 new member states and 75 million new EU citizens. Five decades after our great project of European integration began, we are celebrating the fact that Europeans are no longer kept apart by artificial ideological barriers.'
Romano Prodi, EU Commission President, May 01 2004

*O*utside, the sound of straining brakes interrupts the quiet of the Tuesday rain. I get up and close the curtains, shutting out the damp deckchairs and the London roofs. I press Play. For a moment there is darkness and silence, then a blurred peach haze. I feel my eyes squint and my heart tighten. The camera is shaky as it pulls out. The haze becomes an ankle. Nothing moves. I sit and stare at the screen.

The car pulls out, speeding in front of a tram. She looks back for one final glimpse of the Palace for Culture and Science.

'An impressive example of cold war penis envy,' she says.

He smiles. 'Were you the group that filmed this?'

'No, we did that crude before-and-after thing: the old milk bar with the communist newspapers, and then that giant glass jungle of a media building. Poland today, spanning two worlds, you know the type of thing. It was hardly rocket science.' She pauses. 'What did you think of them?'

'What, the films? Some were good; some were awful. But you hardly had any time, right?'

'Four days.'

'Yeah, I mean four days, what can you do in four days?'

'Anyway it's a weird situation, all of us trying to make films about Poland, which we know nothing about, in no time. We weren't expecting actual students of the film school to come along though. Very embarrassing.'

He glances over to see if she is blushing, but no, her thin face is as pale as ever, her scraped-back hair accentuating her sharp features. She looks from another time, he thinks. She has an eighteenth-century nose, perhaps a slightly cruel nose. He realises she is asking him a question.

'Yes, I was born and bought up there; I kind of commute to Warsaw – back to Kraków at weekends.'

They are out in the suburbs now, low buildings, parks and the tramlines fading. Then, seamlessly, the conversation stops and the talking begins. They talk and talk, past the small towns, the oversized power plants and the empty countryside. They talk through the forests, the valleys and the billboards. They stop to buy tiny, sweet forest strawberries from the roadside as the sun sets. It is as ridiculously romantic as it sounds, and he has stopped making character judgements from the shape of her nose and has become lost in the sound of her words. She looks out the window as they talk and wants to touch him, to put her hand on his thigh, or brush his arm with hers.

Now it is a leg. In the warm, dark light I can see the hairs. I feel my lungs contract and I involuntarily take a deep breath. The camera pans out and keeps moving, slowly up the thigh (the body is on its side) and onto the buttock, where it stops. Suddenly, I hear a noise downstairs and press Stop. *Daytime TV fills the room and I fumble with the control to silence it. I run over to the stairwell. Stillness. There is nothing. 'Hello,' I call. Silence. I press* Play *again, turning up the volume.*

By the time they get to Kraków Airport they have talked about films, poetry, self-doubt and politics. They disagree about films, find some common ground in poetry, and are in complete agreement on self-doubt and politics. They have stopped in the car park. She is low in her seat, knees up against the dashboard, finishing off the strawberries and talking. He has turned in his seat to look at her. She finishes her sentence and glances at him and grins. He smiles back at her. Something has happened on the road between Warsaw and Kraków on this July afternoon, and neither quite knows what it is.

'I really should go – I'm going to miss the flight.'

They get out, into the warm night. She inhales deeply and then scans the car for her possessions, absent-mindedly picking up bits of strawberry.

'I'm fine, you don't need to come in.' She puts the case onto its wheels. 'Thanks, thanks for the lift; it was really kind. So, see you.'

She awkwardly kisses him on the cheek. They hug, each surreptitiously breathing the smell of the other.

She turns to walk away and then twists round, and sees him still there, bulky in his black corduroy jacket. 'Of course, if you are ever in London, you're welcome to stay.'

She walks away, buoyant and light. Nothing can reach her. When they charge her for excess baggage she smiles and pays without complaint. She contentedly gazes at the wall as they announce the delay to her flight, replaying the past six hours in her mind. As they fly over Belgium, she remembers his smell.

Jerkily, the camera pans out, and suddenly the whole back is visible, curving up out of the frame. I can almost feel the skin. There is the protruding mole, which hurts when touched. Suddenly I get cramped by nausea and press Pause. I realise I am crying. The room is silent. I walk to the window, push open the curtains and press my face against the glass. After a few minutes I turn back to the huge screen. Stretched from the ceiling to the banister, the paused image jumps so it almost looks as though the torso on screen is gyrating. I turn away.

He looks different here: a tall stranger dazed amongst the underwear and fast food in Liverpool Street Station. She sees him from a distance and is tempted to turn away. He is looking around; suddenly he seems vulnerable, and she is scared. She keeps walking towards him, long confident strides.

They skirt the shining towers, winding their way through narrow streets and curry shops to a noisy bar full of asymmetrical haircuts and plastic earrings. He tells her about his graduation film; she tells him about a recent documentary festival. They drink through the awkwardness, which follows them into the bedroom. Neither is sure what the other thinks; two weeks of earnest emails followed by suggestive texts make for a clumsy reunion. She sits on the bed. He begins to unpack his bag. Rooting around, he produces a bottle of vodka. She squeals in thanks. He stands up and looks around him.

Ella Saltmarshe | 137

'Come here,' she says, 'you're making me nervous.' He sits down; she leans over and they kiss.

I realise I've been staring at the gyrating image for a while, drinking my tea, transfixed by the epileptic movement.

Jacek decides to stay, charming his way into advertising. He films the *New Visions* researcher asking students what they think of glow-in-the-dark alcopops, mothers their opinions of Burger King, and young professionals why they don't take holidays in Florida. The one thing *New Visions* doesn't ask for is any form of documentation from their freelance cameraman.

She, having been temporarily distracted by love, continues to find that her documentaries about poverty/climate change/refugees do not resonate with the commissioning editors. Soon Jacek is paying most of the rent on the Bethnal Green flat and she is temping at a local college.

Jacek settles easily in the city, has been short-listed for film school and is liked. A teacher of his once said, 'I shouldn't tell you this, but if you have a strong narrative and engaging characters, the audience won't notice technical inconsistencies.' The same goes for Jacek in London; people are so caught up in his momentum that they don't notice the lack of a P45 form, his constant inability to do overseas jobs and his nervousness whenever the police are near.

It is February 2004. He has been here for eighteen months and only has to stall for another two before he will be legal.

The tape is still playing and suddenly his face fills the frame. The eyes are shut, the mouth slightly turned down. His wide forehead, the milk spots by his eyes, the long nose and then those pert lips. I can almost smell his night breath. The lips move closer and closer. The lens mists.

She comes back from the toilet, shivering. It is a cold February night. They have fallen asleep with the light on and she reaches to turn it off, but then stops. He looks beautiful on the bed, in the soft light. She goes out to find the camera and starts to film. She pans up and down his body. Having filmed his back, she clumsily climbs over him, recording his arms, his chest, his face. She stops and moves closer and closer until the lens is almost touching his lips, and then pulls back.

He blinks, opens his eyes. 'What the fuck are you doing?'

'Filming you, asleep.'

'Why? What the fuck? Turn if off.'

'I just wanted you on film, that's all, you looked so nice.'

He rolls over.

Of course there is something wrong, she knows, though she doesn't know she knows. She is grasping, clutching at him, already preparing for a time without him. He can feel it, like sharp fingernails digging in, and it just makes him want to leave faster.

I get up and pull the phone book off the shelf.

The whole thing is like some cheap film. He has a bottle of Jack Daniels in one hand. She is crying. He gets up and puts his coat on.

She cries, 'Don't go, please don't go; stay.'

He says, 'No, I can't.'

She is sitting on the floor and reaches over to hold his leg. 'Stay, please stay.' Suddenly she realises what she is doing, briefly finds some reserve of dignity and releases him.

'I won't let you go,' she says. She sees he is crying, and mistakes his tears for remorse, but these are Jack Daniel tears. She runs in front of him and puts her back to the door. 'Will you fucking let me leave,' he shouts, 'I've got to go.' He lifts her away and walks out. She stands in the doorway, shouting his name, but Jacek does not look back.

The lens has been wiped clean, though it is still misty and some of the dust from the sheet has stuck to it. His whole face is in the image; his eyes open and he looks straight into the camera, confusion and fear moving imperceptibly into anger.

I press Pause and can feel the fury growing, and I know what I have to do. It is the obvious thing. I might be reeling from weeping, no sleep and a drought of a hangover, but I'm clear about what comes next. I look at the date, February 24th; there's still time.

I pick up the phone and dial; a woman answers. I hear my own voice speaking, familiar, clear, unwavering. 'Hello, yes, I'd like to report an illegal immigrant – no, no – I don't want to give my name-his name is Jacek Pieta. He is staying at 42 Littlebury Gardens, Clapham. He works for New Visions in Kensington. He is from Poland.' I hang up before they ask any more questions.

It was so easy. Suddenly I am petrified. I have never done anything like this before. I make serious documentaries and last Saturday marched against the war. I am a good person.

His face is still on the screen. I open the curtains and the image dissolves in the light.

Justine Shaw

Johann Tossick and his Case of Socks

As Johann Tossick awoke one morning from uneasy dreams, he found himself transformed in his bed into a rather slight businessman. Having gone to sleep the night before in an anxious state – his morning thoughts were calm – he suddenly felt quite happy.

He knew, although he couldn't quite remember how he knew it, but he knew that he had to meet a client, a man who lived in the centre of Prague, and that there might be a possibility that this man wanted to buy some socks – lots of socks.

Johann threw back his sheets and lowered his feet onto the cold stone floor. He dashed through the unheated apartment to his bathroom. After turning on the bath taps, he caught sight of a young male looking out from the mirror – he went closer and stared hard as steam began to cloud the room. Placing one hand on his head, he let it rebound softly from the dark curls. 'Who could resist those curls?' his grandmother used to say. 'Who indeed?' he said out loud.

Johann was impatient for the warmth of the water and got into the bath while it was still shallow, letting it fill around him. He sank under the water and thought through his sock range: wool, silk, cashmere in every colour from coal to diamond. His client was in for a treat.

Looking the part was, of course, very important and he started to envisage his attire for the day. Blue suit, brown shoes, white shirt – he suddenly longed for the crispness of his cold, white shirt – and then his yellow tie. He'd wear cashmere taupe socks.

Johann dressed and walked out into the hallway where he picked up a very dusty sock case. He smacked it hard and repeatedly until the hallway was full of dust. Quickly, he opened the door, thankful for the fresh air of the deserted stairwell. It was the first time he had left the flat in over a year.

He walked out onto the street. The weak sun had carved a silver hollow in a white sky. There would be snow later. Burying his hands in his coat pockets, Johann caressed the fur lining. He could see children skating and throwing snowballs across the frozen Vltava. The cold air bit his face and he felt happy to be alive.

His tram arrived quickly. He smiled at the driver's ear. 'Such a nice day.'

The driver turned his eyes away from the road and looked at his passenger. Not a single person had been so chirpy in over a year. 'Mr Tossick! Welcome back! Good morning. You've been away such a long time.'

'Yes, yes, Mr Petrokov, I've had a long time away, but I'm back now.'

'Where have you been?'

Johann Tossick stared at the tram driver and the tram driver stared back at him. 'I mustn't keep you, Mr Petrokov. These people' – Johann nodded to his fellow passengers – 'have jobs to get to.'

'Yes yes.' And, with that, the tram trundled into the centre of Prague, carrying Johann Tossick and his case of socks.

His client's house was near the tram stop. Johann walked briskly and arrived within a minute. He knocked and a sleepy man opened the door.

'Mr Tossick' – first slowly and then the realisation – 'Mr Tossick, you're' – an intake of breath and then incredulously – 'you're a year late!'

'And an hour early,' replied the effervescent Johann.

'Mr Tossick, I see you've brought...' His client looked down at the sock case and then back to Johann's face and said, still evidently stunned, 'You've brought the socks.'

'Yes. Everyone needs socks.'

'Yes, but I have plenty, and I am no longer in the sock trade. I've decided to concentrate on my writing.'

'Oh, oh,' said Johann. 'May I come in?' Snow was starting to fall and he was feeling cold.

'Yes. But only for five minutes. I really must write. And please' – he grabbed hold of Johann's arm in a manner that Johann felt was somewhat inappropriate – 'please don't try to sell me any socks.'

The man led Johann into his study and a clock chimed eight times. A teapot sat on a small table that had an armchair on either side of it. His host ran to the kitchen and called back to his houseguest, 'I'll get you a cup and perhaps you'd like some strudel?'

'Thank you,' Johann called back as he sank down into one of the armchairs. Now might just be the right time for a little breakfast, he thought to himself.

The man came back with two cups and two slices of raisin-addled strudel. He suddenly seemed quite buoyed to have company and appeared eager to chat to his old acquaintance, the travelling sock salesman.

'So tell me, what's been happening? Where have you been the last year?'

Johann took a deep breath. 'Well, Mr Kafka,' he began, 'one morning I awoke from uneasy dreams to find myself transformed...'

Katherine May

Swallowed

L et me describe the scene to you. I'm sitting at the kitchen table, letting my supper go cold. Michael, my youngest, has gone to bed, and Joanna, who barely counts as a child any more, is in her room playing her guitar. I'm going to have to tell her to keep it down in a minute; it's getting late. The neighbours will be cross again, but I don't really care - not now. I don't think we'll be neighbours for much longer.

In front of me is a wide, white plate upon which a beautiful meal has been set out: pork fillets, stuffed with sage, prosciutto and fontina cheese, with puy lentils and wine gravy. With it there's broad beans dressed with mint and olive oil - out of season, but never mind that - I've spotted dessert in the fridge: crème brûlée with a seam of raspberries along the bottom, and a bottle of Sauternes to go with it.

I'm sure it's delicious, but I'll have to take it on faith, because all I've managed so far is to chase it around my plate with the tip of my knife. Robert's sitting opposite me, head hung low over his meal, and he's shovelling, I mean, literally, shovelling it, flat-forked, in to his rat-trap of a mouth. And every time his jaw snaps shut, I can hear an accompanying gulp of air getting swallowed down, and I can see the wattled skirts of flesh around his neck shudder.

I can barely force down my wine.

My children, I would have to say, are the most clear-skinned I've seen. Jo may hide hers in a fug of fag-smoke and eyeliner, but she glows, she really does. She's a credit to me, to the efforts I've made over the years, although she'd never admit to it.

I've been outmoded, you see; I'm a dirty secret; I'm everything a young girl aspires not to be.

I'm a housewife. Not a worn-down social security refugee who spends the day watching hyperbolic chat shows, for whom not working, rather than housewifery, is the highest aspiration; nor some grudging career-woman, whose ambitions have been crushed under the weight of her own fertility. No, I am a housewife by choice, and by profession.

It's an art-form, keeping house; done right, it has an elegance about it, a symmetry. It is about imposing order on the chaos of family life, harnessing the whims and energies of those in your care, and manipulating them into something wholesome, organised, fruitful. It's a wonderful thing, a well-maintained family.

But that's also bollocks. I mean, I'm sure a well-maintained family is a thing to behold, but I have no idea, as mine resembles...well, I don't know what. A group of people who have nothing in common other than a shared roof over their heads, I suppose.

But at least the children have got that glow about them. It's the food, you know. Too many people these days feed their children utter crap. You see it in the supermarket: sinister faces made from reformed poultry, cartons of composite ham and plastic cheese masquerading as lunch, and everything covered in those chemical-orange breadcrumbs. You've only got to read the ingredients list. There's no real food anywhere in these products, just a list of e-numbers.

It's not simply that we are what we eat, although that's true enough. No, food is more than its nutritional value; good food has something purifying about it; it resets to zero the evils of the world outside. I've always believed that my soups and stews are like family glue, that I'm implanting, layer by layer, the right way of life into their rumbling stomachs.

I made a new friend, about a month ago. It's funny; you're constantly meeting new people when you're young, but once you've had kids, it's like the outside world recedes. The only new people I've met in years have been mothers at the school gates, and a few of them have been round for dinner, but it's never worked out.

Anyway, a new deli opened up in the village about a month ago. A lovely job's been done of it too: it's all tiles and marble, with a little bar at the end where you can sit and drink a cappuccino with deep, silky froth. Everything's Italian, and I found myself in awe the first time I stepped in. There were great hairy legs of wild boar prosciutto, jars of huge capers with long stalks, globes of buffalo mozzarella floating serenely in earthenware bowls, and everywhere this air of calm capability.

I've hit it off a bit with the woman who runs it. She's called Maria, but she's not an Italian herself – apparently she used to be married to one. I'd normally have given her a wide berth – she's got an unkempt look about her, and I'm not sure I like that near to food – but seeing as I was in for a cappuccino most mornings we ended up getting to know one another, and after a while I found myself going in there just to laugh along with her.

When I'm in there, it feels like everything's under control, which is how I used to feel about home, but not any longer. It's all changed.

Food was always my thing, right from the start, before the children even. I can remember how it felt, the day after I moved in, when Robert left at eight to go to the surgery, and I stood, for an hour, in the quiet hallway, listening to the whir of the washing machine and the grave chat on the radio, and watching the dust drift past the stained glass in the front door; and I felt utterly empty: not happy, not sad, just nothing.

And, you see, I realised I had to make a role for myself, to do something useful, because you could go mad in all that quiet. So I went out into the garden, and picked the blackberries from the bramble at the bottom of the lawn, and some damsons from the tree by the kitchen window, and I made two types of jam. And then I walked into the village and bought a brace of fat pork chops, and a bag of potatoes and some runner beans from the greengrocer's, and I laid the table and starched him a shirt for the morning, and all of these things were ready when he came home.

And it's been the same ever since. Every night, without fail, Robert has come home to a plate of food that is delicious, nourishing, produced from the finest ingredients and above all, home-made.

I can recall the stab of joy when, in the first year of our marriage, he would descend on the dinner table with the vigour of a man with much earthier things on his mind; in fact, I think my meals used to implant ideas in him, because, after he had eaten the meal in quiet reverence, emitting regular, soft grunts of delight, he would sweep me up in his arms, and kiss me, and say, what did I do to deserve the most beautiful wife in the world?

He's never wanted for a thing. I have risen early every morning so that he has a hearty breakfast inside him when he tackles his morning rounds: porridge with brown sugar and raspberries, free-range eggs with thick rashers of streaky bacon, American pancakes with maple syrup. And every day he has a proper packed lunch: perhaps cold chicken and salad with home-made mayonnaise, or a sandwich of crusty bread with ham from the bone and hot English mustard, and always, always, without fail, a little note on his paper napkin that says, I love you.

I still write those notes, but it's only out of habit, really. If I stopped sending them it would be a sign, wouldn't it? It would be a deliberate withdrawal, in effect a note saying, I don't love you any more.

It would be true though. I don't.

The children were both breast-fed, of course. I watched all of the women in the mother and baby group that I set up rush their babies onto formula milk, and then onto those gelatinous jars of food that claim to encapsulate a full steak and kidney dinner into half-a-cup of whitish goo. So I breast-fed, somewhat heroically given the state of my nipples, for at least a month longer than everyone else, by which time I had achieved nigh-on cult status amongst the group for my perseverance, and then I seamlessly switched to an array of puréed fruits and vegetables.

Beautiful, they were, gem-coloured: pale yellow apple, rich orange sweet potato, dazzling green pea and mint. There's a special pleasure in children's food. I always wanted mine to eat storybook foods, Enid Blyton cooking: dippy eggs and neat soldiers; bread and honey; a proper roast every Sunday with crumble or pie for pudding. I dug a vegetable patch at the bottom of the garden, and we grew peas, carrots, marrows (although heaven knows why), potatoes, beetroot, lettuces; you name it, we went down and got our wellies muddy in order to bring it to the table. I've given them proper butter, always, and full-cream milk.

The problem is that it sounds more perfect than it actually was. For a start, since the age of eight Joanna has refused to eat tomatoes. Now, you'd think that this was a minor thing, that one salad vegetable (yes, I know it's really a fruit) would be but a blip on the smooth course of my children's nourishment. But the thing is, it really annoys me. I can't explain it; but then you try getting through an era of Mediterranean-inspired cookery when your daughter won't touch moussaka, Greek salad, pizza and most major forms of pasta sauce. It's embarrassing more than anything: the child stubbornly refuses to eat tomatoes, even when they have been picked fresh from the greenhouse.

And then there's Michael, with his allergies. First it was the asthma, and then the nut allergy (discovered after a peanut butter sandwich at a friend's house, I hasten to add), but now they think he's got a problem with wheat, despite all my years of home-baked bread. It just seems wrong; there's a bit of me that thinks it's more of a rebellion than anything, but I suppose it's not his fault.

More and more, I feel that they're all conspiring against me, the three of them. Jo with her boyfriends and cigarettes and that sneer that freezes her face whenever I speak to her; Michael with his aches and pains and his scraping the bottom of second-set maths; and Robert, well, for Robert just being there does for me these days.

Twenty years, it's been; four without the children, and sixteen with. And for nineteen years I was satisfied with this life, but not any longer. I suppose our marriage has been in decline for years, but it's only recently that I've seen it as something to worry about.

As I've said, at the beginning he would descend on each morsel I served up with murmurs of pleasure; he used to thank me for every last scrap. Over the years, his praise has become less forthcoming. I have learned to watch for clues as to the level of his enjoyment: the last smear of mashed potato rounded up on his knife and licked off; the request for a piece of bread to mop up the sauce.

Lately, it's got worse. My packed lunches are being returned untouched, and I've been finding sweet wrappers in his pockets. He's partial to a Snickers, apparently; that's news to me. I wonder if he even notices the food I put down in front of him at night, or whether it's just another reason for him not to speak to me.

When the kids came along, everything changed; it always does. They're like little sponges, kids: they sop up every last drop of your attention, and leave you with nothing else. When it first occurred to me that Robert was getting complacent, I thought, so what? I've got other people to care for now. When they were tiny, it was enough to be wiping dribbles of food from their faces; later, I was busy with seeing them off to school in the morning and then getting ready for when they got home.

By the time they were getting too old for my fussing, I realised that not having to take part in the world was enough for me. I've seen what it does to you: Robert has these morose lines that have faded onto his forehead over the years, which he tries to iron out with the pads of his fingers. All I want out of life is to be able to cling to the world in which I can take my time to watch the sun filtering through the kettle smoke in the afternoons, and to smell the first hit of hot water on tea. That's enough. Or rather, it was enough.

I've come to see my cooking as a Sisyphean labour. Just as Sisyphus was condemned to eternally roll a rock up a hill, only to watch helpless as it rolled back down, so I feel condemned to produce ever more elaborate meals, only to watch them be thoughtlessly consumed by my family, or worse, picked at disgustedly, as I have seen Jo do. In my mind's eye, the kids have become nothing but a set of insatiable, obliterating jaws, and Robert has become a wanton destroyer of the things I love, my little creations.

Robert's got fat on my hard work. I watched him undress last night; it was the first time I've really looked at him for a long time, and he's vile, I mean utterly revolting. He's a clammy white all over, and his nipples hang pendulously, like they're about to blossom into fully-fledged breasts. His chest hairs are turning grey, and his navel is stretched as if it's weeping with the strain of punctuating his flaccid gut.

Maria's garden is full of weeds; her house is full of clutter. When she invited me round, on a Wednesday afternoon about a month ago, I had to shift a pile of newspapers off the sofa before I could sit on it.

She offered me gin, and I asked for tea instead, and then I chased her into the kitchen and told her I'd changed my mind. We drank the whole bottle, sitting on her cracked patio, and we talked about everything: her hopes for the deli, my work on the village fête committee, her divorce, the state of my marriage. And that was it; it was like unknotting a balloon – everything just sailed out, and tore around the space between us, things I'd never even thought before, but which now I believed, about Robert and his deadening belief that marriage is something which is achieved, once, and which never needs attention again, and how I've got so frightened about the world that all I do is follow little patterns, every day, and how I've raised two complacent, bourgeois brats, and that, and that...

And Maria stroked my hair and my face and she kissed me.

When I got home that afternoon, the answer phone was bleeping. It was the headmistress at the kids' school, ringing to say that some child or other had reported Michael for bullying. I rang back and arranged a time to come in and I made all the right noises (although it was hard trying not to slur), and then I put myself to bed, and I lay there thinking, of course my son's a bully. Why would he be anything else?

The world's moved on, and I'm the last one to know. All of a sudden, I'm a bad mother, I'm a drain on their independence, I'm a poor example to my daughter and a nurturer of my over-privileged son's ego. I'm a prop to a bunch of complacent little shits, their father included, who barely register that I'm alive.

I haven't cooked since. The kids didn't even notice at first. When I ordered in pizza and Chinese and kebabs, they put their righteous heads down, just the same, and ate it. But Robert did. He ate it quietly for the first couple of nights, and then he asked if everything was alright, and then he said he had to 'raise an objection' about what he was being fed, and so I gave him the menus and let him order his supper for himself.

The day after, he asked if I was ill, and a few days after that he just put his head on the table and sobbed and sobbed, and said that he was sorry and that he'd make it right. And I just stood and watched, and I couldn't even bear to touch him.

Tonight when I came in from Maria's, he had cooked me supper. And it's beautiful, I told you that already. He's lapping it up, poor soul; he's not eaten properly for weeks. But I can't eat a thing; I've got Maria on my mind, and the meals she feeds me – bacon sandwiches in bed, fish and chips in their wrapper, rice pudding from the tin – and the feeling of those papers crinkling under my naked back on the sofa, and the rasp of the soles of her feet on my shins, and the black stains around her tired eyes.

I'm leaving. I've raised a husband and I've serviced a pair of children, and

I don't want any of them any more. They've been poor recipients of my attentions; they don't deserve me.

I don't know even what I'm going to do, but I shall start with the dark ring around Maria's bathtub, and I shall work my way outwards from there.

Leslie
Mapp

The Limits of Friendship

A délaide liked people to visit her by train. If they sat on the left, then just before they reached the station, they would get the best view of her building. They would see the decorated brickwork and the two plaster sphinxes that sat defending the entrance. If visitors came by car, all they saw were the mean, pinched buildings that had crowded round since the old apartment-house was built. Then, there had been a real village here, not just the remnants of a name on the city plan. Then, the flag-stones on which the recycling bins now lurked had been a green, where young ladies had wheeled in their bustles, proud to be newly employed in London, the optimistic heart of the Empire, a short ride away on the new railway. These women had felt liberated by Mr Remington's iron typewriter. In their enthusiasm, they had flooded into company offices, feeling contemporary and alive, some living proudly in this apartment-building for single women that had sprung up to provide an appropriate modesty.

By the time Adélaide reached her own desk one hundred years later, the office was no longer a place of daring and promise, it had become a drudgery of the worst kind. Born in France, Adélaide had left home early to escape a love affair. Everyone in her village had approved the match, but she knew it was destined to end in marriage or suicide, and she didn't want either of those things. She had come, eventually, to this building because she appreciated its beauty - and because it was cheap now to rent in this unfashionable quarter. But today was Saturday and she was not working; she was standing at her front window, drinking from a small glass of orange-juice, and looking out to the railway over the flat roofs of the warehouses opposite, waiting for Tom's train to appear. He would see her, and their day would begin with a meeting of eyes across this space.

She saw the train, and stared into the windows of the second carriage. Tom's eyes looked back. She imagined the smile on his face so she also smiled. Without apparent change in her demeanour, she turned from the window, unlatched the apartment door, and took her glass into the bedroom. She lay back on a pillow with a sigh; a visceral anticipation of comfort that only the next few hours ever contained so entirely. It wasn't that she loved Tom, but she loved something that he brought; an uncomplicated mood that made her feel more alive for the time they were together. She didn't know much more about him than this, but it was enough to make the minutes stretch as she waited for him to arrive. Beneath a yawn of anticipation she prepared herself, hips pressing down into the bedcover, arms lying mute by her side.

The front door shut and Tom appeared in the bedroom doorway, throwing his jacket across a chair. Adélaide closed her eyes. She felt Tom's weight fall down beside her. His breathing came close and he put his mouth into her hair. She rolled towards him and let herself float to the sound of a freight train rumbling through the station, its containers clanking emptily down the line on their way back over the sea to China. For an hour they became the same person, then they separated into their two skins, still keeping very close; and sometime after that, Tom looked into her eyes and spoke softly – 'Hello you' – and they slowly dissolved into their two beings.

'I may be sent to Belgium,' said Tom, sliding an arm under her head and pressing himself against her back.

'When?'

'Soon, for about a year. Will you come?'

'Yes,' said Adélaide, 'it will be nice to visit.'

'No,' said Tom, 'I mean will you come with me to Belgium?'

Adélaide felt very naked. 'You don't want me to,' she said at last, unsure of what this meant.

'Yes, I do,' said Tom. 'I heard about the Belgium job months ago. As soon as I heard I thought of asking you to come, if I got it. The company flat is set up for two; I'm sure they won't mind if I take someone.'

'Why didn't you say anything before?'

'Because I didn't know I'd get the job,' said Tom, 'and I didn't want to disappoint you.'

'But I am disappointed now,' said Adélaide, 'because you didn't tell me.' She sat up in the bed, and looked down into Tom's face, his smile only slightly dimmed by her last comment.

'Come with me,' he said. 'It will be good.'

Adélaide picked her glass from the bedside table and tipped it back until it was drained. She reached for her dressing gown. 'I'll make some tea,' she said. 'Assam or Ceylon?'

'Coffee!' shouted Tom into the room, reaching back and ragging on a window-curtain. 'I want Belgian coffee and Belgian chocolates and then some blonde beer in a restaurant lined with wild boars' heads. And I want you to be there with me.'

Adélaide slipped into the kitchen. Her flat still retained some original interior and she looked upward now at the plaster fruit on the ceiling, searching for how she felt. She knew that Tom wasn't proposing marriage, but a year with him in Belgium seemed almost the same thing. As the water heated, she warmed three croissants in the oven. One of them was often extra hungry on Saturday mornings.

'Thank you, Tom,' said Adélaide as she put the tray on the bed, 'but I don't think I want to leave London.'

'Adéle, you've got to come!' said Tom, 'I've planned it now.'

'Planned what?' said Adélaide. 'Why haven't you told me any of this before?'

'I wanted it to be a surprise,' said Tom, lowering his voice a little and adding with less certainty, 'a nice surprise.'

'This is not fair,' said Adélaide. 'You've made these plans, but told me nothing about them. How can I just leave and go to Belgium? I don't know anyone there or anything about it.'

'You'll know me,' said Tom with a smile. 'Isn't that a start?'

'I can't just spend a year with you,' said Adélaide, pulling tight the cord on her gown.

Tom looked away to the window, and stared out at the blue, summer sky. Adélaide watched him put his cup to his lips and flinch slightly at the heat against his skin. She knew he would taste it with care; he'd complained before about her unusual choice of infusions. The sound of metal shutters being run open in the warehouse across the road broke his silence.

'Adélaide,' he said carefully, 'I don't want to go alone; please come with me. I know we're not in love, but I thought it would work – you and I on a long holiday. The company are expecting you to go now.'

'The company?' said Adelaide, an anger rising up inside her. 'You've already told the company?'

'I asked. I wanted to make sure it would be alright,' said Tom. 'I didn't know.'

'Didn't know?' said Adelaide. 'Of course you didn't know, you didn't ask me. So now everyone in the company knows about your plans and I'm supposed to play along. "Oh, Adélaide will come," you must have said to them, "she'll be grateful for anything!"'

'It wasn't like that,' said Tom, suddenly louder. 'I didn't want to disappoint you. And I don't think of you as "poor Adélaide"!'

Furious now, Adélaide pointedly held her stare into his eyes, and saw Tom gather himself against the pull of a corresponding emotion.

'Adéle,' he said steadily, 'this is becoming a problem. These days I don't know how to speak to you.'

'What do you mean?' said Adélaide, surprised at the way the words sounded, strangled and angry and tearful.

'I know we only see each other now and then,' Tom went on, 'but you've been different lately. You don't seem so patient, or...I don't know, so "here". What's wrong?'

'I don't know what you're talking about,' said Adélaide. 'I haven't been any different.'

'There's been a film over your eyes,' said Tom. 'I don't even know if you know it.'

Adélaide looked at Tom. Under her stare, he made an uncomfortable gesture with his hand, which she interpreted as him moving in her direction and she retreated almost imperceptibly away. She didn't know if he had noticed this.

'I'm not going to Belgium,' said Adélaide suddenly. 'I'll visit, but I'm not going to live there.'

'What's wrong?' repeated Tom, reaching for her across the bed, scattering the croissants from the plate across the cover.

For a moment, Adélaide's muscles resisted his pull, but with little outward sign they began to relax into his embrace, not assuaging her fury but holding it between her and the touch of his skin. Tom kissed the top of her head and placed his hand gently on her breast, in a sign more of benediction than of sex.

'What's wrong?' he said for the third time.

Adélaide sighed; she knew Tom was right. Like a ripple through water, something had passed by. Recently she'd felt only an absence of feeling, which had begun to nag; not even the summer sun had touched the smallest part of her. Slowly, with a careful affection, she felt Tom begin to speak the only language they really shared. He moved his hand lightly against her breast and stretched his length along hers so they were touching from lips to feet.

Their love-making suited them well; they'd discovered this a little while after they met. One day, discussing the limits of friendship, they had pushed against them, and an hour later were in bed together. They'd continued the habit, although, apart from this intimacy, they'd made no plans for creating more. They were two people who enjoyed each other's company now and then at a film or a play, but more often in bed. Anything closer than this was too near. In the months of their friendship's new boundary, they had neither argued nor spent a whole night together. Now, unlike the first sex of the morning, they separated easily into their two selves.

'What's the time?' asked Tom, rolling himself up in the sheets and stretching like a dog dreaming in the sunshine.

'Just after one,' said Adélaide, reaching over to the clock on the bedside table.

'I told you I had to leave by three today?' said Tom, with a complicated out-breath that included several underlying harmonies of sound.

'Yes,' said Adélaide. 'You're meeting Lee before the concert.'

'I'll make some coffee,' said Tom, lurching ungainly onto the carpet and stretching some more, 'black or white?'

'White,' said Adélaide, 'but I'll get it if you like.'

'Don't worry,' said Tom. 'I'll make it.' He pulled his trousers up from the floor and over his legs, and slipped his T-shirt over his head.

As she listened to the sounds from the kitchen, Adélaide moved around the bedroom, gathering clothes for the rest of her day. Tom switched on the radio. She chose a mauve suede skirt and a green jumper, with her favourite green boots. Even though she knew these would be too warm, she liked the idea of encasing her legs in their fur and laces. She draped the clothes over the mirror and placed the boots near the door. She was doing this as Tom returned with the coffee.

'What are you doing today?' he said, putting the new cups next to the old ones on the tray.

'Meeting Lynne and Marco in the park,' she said. 'We're going to a film.'

'Which one?' he said.

'The Japanese one at the arts club,' she replied. 'I've heard it's very good.'

The coffee tasted good and they rescued pieces of croissant from the bed, laughing as they fed each other crumbs. Another clanking freight train went by outside. They talked easily of other things, but at last Tom said quietly, 'I suppose we'll forget about Belgium.'

'I'll visit', said Adélaide, sure of her reply, and embracing him in an unspoken communication.

Tom slipped from between her arms and bent to find his shoes.

'I'll call you later,' he said, easing his jacket off the chair and over his shoulders. 'Perhaps we can see a movie next week.'

By the front door, he put both hands on her shoulders and pressed them inward as if they were in danger of dropping off. She hunched her back and they made the ritual kissing of cheeks they always did in ironic recognition of her Continental origins, but also as an unconscious remaking of their individual distance. Tom let himself out.

Adélaide turned back into the room and picked up a stray shoe. She took it into the bedroom and lay down with it on the bed. She held it against herself and felt the hardness of the heel against her chest. She looked up at the ceiling. Then she got up and started to tidy the sheets where she and Tom had lain. Suddenly, with a fierce motion, she pulled them all off the bed and threw them into a pile on the floor. Then she lay down again and her nostrils filled with the rough smell of the mattress. She watched the afternoon shadow cross the ceiling and she marvelled at its speed. How could the sun be moving so quickly through the days when her heart had remained so still through all these years?

Rob
Sears

Double Blind Trial

T hat this face is the face of Buchner is not in doubt. We applied scientific method by doubting the face of Buchner.

The test was a double blind trial, which meant a Buchner lookalike had to be hired with a different face. Students and cleaning staff were then paid to identify Buchner. Some picked Buchner. Some picked the lookalike. One picked Professor Delorney, who was using the laboratory as a through route. We told subject to pick again but subject refused. We ran the test again with Professor Delorney as a third option and the results were confounding. There is a real possibility she has Buchner's face.

In the first run, no one picked the lab assistant, who was standing to the right of Buchner and the lookalike. Buchner had put her there as a dummy third option to mix things up a little. But no one identified her as him and the lab assistant dropped out in favour of Professor Delorney when, as described, a subject identified the latter.

After the second run, Albretto and I convened with our funders. Result: the lab assistant will receive tenure next year in disguise as Professor Delorney.

That Buchner lied under oath about the hit-and-run is beyond doubt. He told us so in the local. We were in the local and Buchner came out with it. But it is our job to doubt everything. We applied game theory to discover whether he was lying then, in the local not under oath, or whether he had been lying before, in the chambers under oath. The lab assistant disguised as Professor Delorney pretended to be the child. Albretto pretended to be Buchner's car. Albretto took Professor Delorney on his shoulders and ran into the lab assistant disguised as Professor Delorney. Then Albretto ran from the scene of the crime, still with Buchner on his shoulders.

The object was to make Buchner relive his crime. If he relived the hit-and-run and broke down, then he had lied in the chambers and told the truth in the local. If he failed to relive the crime and remained standing, then he had told the truth in the chambers and lied in the local.

Albretto ran around the corner with Buchner on his shoulders. When we caught up with them Buchner was standing. But Albretto said that Buchner had broken down and recovered in the space of a minute. The conclusion was that Buchner had lied in the chambers under oath. Alternatively, we could doubt Albretto's claim that Buchner had broken down around the corner.

Then we found someone tied up in the washroom. Albretto degagged him. He said he was the real Buchner, and the lookalike Buchner had tied him up and faked a breakdown to make it look as if he, the real Buchner, had lied in the chambers. It was a fit-up, the real Buchner said. Albretto looked at me and I looked at Albretto. If this was the real Buchner, we still didn't know if he had lied in the chambers or in the local. If this was an impostor, and the real Buchner had broken down on Albretto's shoulders, then we knew it was in the chambers that the real Buchner had lied. And if this was an impostor, and Albretto's claim that the real Buchner had broken down was a lie, then we knew it was in the local that the real Buchner had lied. Alternatively, both Buchners could be impostors.

No one doubts that this is the place of the accident. No one doubts that either Buchner drove here at night and hit the child or he did not, or that the lookalike Buchner did not exist (experimentally) until after the crime. But doubting with us is an ethos. Tenure depends on it.

Though we had not solved the Buchner case, we went to the funders to keep them up to date with our progress. The funders work by committee and were confused by our presentation. They asked us to recreate the accident to help them understand, this time using the real Professor Delorney as the child, Buchner as the car, and Albretto (against his will) as Buchner. We did it this way so the real Buchner did not have to relive his crime in front of the funders and implicate himself (this is part of his Miranda rights). But there was a surprise. Upon hitting Professor Delorney, Albretto broke down. Unlikely as it seemed, we had a new culprit.

Having handcuffed Albretto, Professor Delorney rehearsed the details of my friend's crime. First, Albretto had disguised himself as Buchner, got in Buchner's car and hit a child. Second, dreading the loss of his position, Albretto had let Buchner stand trial. Third, worried that Buchner would be found innocent and another investigation would begin, Albretto had hired the lookalike Buchner to go to the local and admit guilt. He knew we were people of conscience, and would reveal the admission to the judges.

At one point in the aftermath of these deceptions, Albretto, as confused as the funding board about who was under suspicion, had paid Professor Delorney to pretend to be him pretending to be Buchner's car, and he had pretended to be the lookalike Buchner pretending to be the real Buchner on Professor Delorney's shoulders (though none of us had realised that this was who he was supposed to be). Meanwhile, hundreds of AIDS victims were dying every day in South Africa because the therapeutic drugs our team had developed cost too much. Women in the US were working two jobs to pay for breast cancer tests because our funders had patented the best-known method. And in China, litigation had stopped distribution of the world's biggest lifesaver, the TB vaccine. But this last piece of wrangling was outside our control.

Dom
Nemer

Kew

It was a sunny July morning and Robert and Claudine were sitting quietly at the breakfast table – until, that was, Robert spoke. 'My hayfever's flared up,' he said, but Claudine continued to stare at her mug of coffee. So he went back to reading the weekend FT.

'Let's go to Kew Gardens,' said Claudine a moment later.

He put the paper down, looked at her with his red, streaming eyes, and got up to find his shoes.

This sort of exchange was not uncommon in their relationship. Ever since Robert had asked for her hand in marriage, Claudine had done her best to upset him. Robert had done his best *not* to get upset. He believed that her antagonism was a test and that a show of tolerance would please his intended fiancée. The effect, however, was just the opposite; his reactions merely aggravated her and the prospect of saying 'I do' to him grew ever more remote.

At the entrance to Kew she watched as his nose twitched and then ushered him quickly towards the Azalea Garden, knowing full well this would bring on an attack. Along the way he made a point of noticing how beautiful the lilacs looked at this time of year.

When his first sneeze exploded in the Rhododendron Dell, she smiled a smug, perhaps evil smile. To her, the sneeze sounded just like an anguished scream, and she was the architect of that anguish. Robert, however, made light of it. 'Seven more and I'll have had the equivalent of an orgasm,' he said, catching his breath. Claudine's smile vanished – she hadn't had one of those in six months.

This thought plagued her all the way to the Grass Garden, where he sneezed three more times. She watched as he blew his nose and went on to show an interest in the ornamental reeds from southern China. She felt sick with anger. She wanted the sneezing to stop. She wanted to be somewhere else with someone else. She didn't want a boyfriend called Robert. She wanted a life partner called River.

Walking beneath the shady Rose Pergola, she planned out her new life. She would live with River in a beach hut. He would play the bongos and she would write a book called 'Almost a Rainbow'. They would do lots of exciting things together, like swim with barracuda and wear each other's underwear. She needed to get rid of Robert.

Two sneezes later, they reached the Victorian glasshouse, home to endangered island species and carnivorous plants. A plaque at the entrance informed them that Kew had recently made *The Guinness Book of Records* for growing the biggest Venus flytrap in the world, big enough to digest a man. The smile returned to Claudine's face. 'Here I come, River,' she muttered under her breath as Robert let out another sneeze.

Inside, the jungle of palm fronds gave way to a clearing. In the centre of the clearing was the flytrap. Its green shell halves, with their spines like giant eyelashes, were parted to reveal twin cushions of red velvet. 'Beautiful, but deadly,' Robert remarked as they drew nearer. Claudine felt his description of the plant rather matched her persona. She was going to say, 'Why thank you,' in a clever, twisted way; this would make Robert furrow his brow and, in the confusion, give her the chance to despatch him. Instead she screamed.

Wasps had never been a friend to Claudine. One such creature, attracted to the flytrap, was temporarily distracted by the smell of her hairspray. Claudine ran into the palms in an attempt to escape. Robert followed but couldn't keep up. She ran through the flora and back into the clearing, so blinded by fear that she failed to notice the world's largest carnivorous plant rising smack in her path with jaws agape.

Claudine found that she couldn't breathe inside the dark chamber. Nor could her whimpers penetrate the walls that tightened around her. The acidic juices made her skin fizz, then melt, and her intestines fell out. Her body was a simmering, sticky mass that, could it have been seen, looked much like a Thai red curry. The acid took longer to work through her skull. Through holes that once were ears, she was able to hear the sound her stomach made when it popped, allowing her half-digested breakfast to join the bloody omelette.

The last noise she heard before her brain dissolved came from outside. It was an enormous, ground-shaking sneeze. What remained of Claudine seethed with anger, and then regret, and then, finally, nothing.

Adam Elston

Trapped

From the window of the hospital ward Patrick looked out across the road to the rooftop of the flat he had once lived in. He thought about the day he had decided to kill the pigeon trapped in the chimney there and tell his girlfriend he no longer loved her.

He remembered that the two decisions had come to him during the night, simultaneously, while Helen lay sleeping beside him. They emerged with an incontrovertible clarity out of the fog of his insomnia and, his dilemmas resolved, he fell asleep at once. The next morning he awoke and lay still. For a moment he feared that the decisions he had made would be revealed in the light of the day to be foolish and impossible. He need not have worried for, upon examination, both ideas retained that quality that in the night had seemed inspired.

Helen was going out. He remained in bed feigning sleep as she moved around the room and dressed. After a while he heard her pick up her keys and close the door softly behind her. And then the thud of her footsteps on the stairs and then, with a blast of warm air that moved the curtains above his head, she slammed the front door and was gone. He lay for a moment enjoying the peace, listening as the flat, with minute ticks and creaks, adjusted itself to her absence. The sun shone through the windows in the other room and streamed in through the open bedroom door. He lay in its warmth and rested, but then he heard the distant, watery coo of the pigeon that was stuck in the chimney. He sighed and got out of bed.

He dressed, and went through to the other room. Everything seemed radiant in the sunlight. Patrick was grateful for the way Helen kept things in order. The structures she imposed upon their world and the way she appeared to make reality conform to her needs, was, along with her beauty, one of the things that had attracted him to her. It was a complete contrast to the chaos he had experienced growing up. Moving in with Helen meant that he could leave behind the messes and empty cupboards of his childhood. Everything here was in its place. Their two-room flat was small but a massive gilt-edged mirror over the decorative fireplace and the high, corniced ceilings created an illusion of space. There were thick-stemmed red tulips in a vase on the table and the smooth wooden floor shone gold where shafts of sunlight fell upon it.

From the fireplace, a sudden flurry of beating wings broke into the order of the room. The sound was followed by a shower of dust and sooty rubble that were deposited on the floor in front of him. Today, he knew, it would end. He would kill the bird.

After some coffee he climbed the stairs to the top-floor landing and pulled down the ladder to the skylight. He went up and out onto the roof and, once there, stretched with pleasure to feel the sun. It was a beautiful day. The pitch surface of the rooftop was already warm beneath his bare feet. The cars rushing along Euston Road sounded like breaking waves; across the road the green and white panels of the new hospital building glinted like fish scales. He had watched, over months, as the building rose from the ground but he could not pinpoint a moment when it had actually begun to exist. It had happened gradually he thought, moving at a pace too slow to appreciate, the way the hour hand moves around the face of a clock, until one day it was there, existing, complete.

He turned from the street and looked towards the chimneys on top of the parapet in the centre of the roof. When they first heard the cooing and beating of wings they had thought a bird was making a nest, but after his first look a couple of days earlier Patrick knew that this was not the case. He looked into the chimney now and saw the bird sitting glumly on a ledge, only an arm's length down but unable to fly out because of the angle of the shaft above it. Nobody they had called was willing to come out and rescue the pigeon. The professional consensus was that they should wait for it to die and drop into the room below. This course of action, once discussed, had been vetoed by Helen, and Patrick had agreed. They were afraid that the bird would weaken first and drop down alive, flapping its soot and disease around their flat.

His relationship with Helen was nearing the end of its second year and soon they would be leaving university. Some time during the last months – he couldn't determine the specific moment – Patrick had started to feel stifled by the commitment they had made in taking the flat together. He felt that the novelty of their cohabitation – the grown-up sit-down dinners and Sunday morning newspaper sharing – had worn off. Also he felt that he was being continually appraised and sized-up, and he was resentful of the inspection. His decision to end the relationship, and the freedom this would afford him, made him dizzy. But the thought of telling Helen filled him with dread.

The pigeon shifted to adjust its foothold in the soot-darkened gloom of the chimney. Patrick wondered how he would kill it and wondered also if the pigeon sensed that its end was near. He looked around on the roof for something he could use and saw, on the other side of the parapet, a length of plastic pipe he thought might do the job. He got the pipe and climbed back up to the chimney. His idea was to use it to crush or spear the pigeon against the ledge, and then find a way to get the carcass out. But as he held the end of the pipe over the bird, readying himself for the downward stroke, he had an odd sensation. He felt somehow connected to the bird; he could see the nervous twitching of its brittle wings and could sense tiny vibrations of fear rising through the pipe. He thought he could even sense its heartbeat.

As he was about to strike, the pigeon suddenly came out of its trance. Its mad flurry of beating wings startled Patrick so that he nearly fell backwards off the parapet. He cried out and threw the pipe down onto the flat surface of the roof below.

The certainty with which he had awoken was deserting him. He doubted now that he could go ahead with his plan – but he knew the pigeon could not stay in there forever. He walked to where the pipe had landed and, nearby, found a length of thin blue nylon rope. He picked up the rope, thought for a moment, and then folded it in two and fed it down the length of pipe until it appeared at the other end. He now had a noose. With renewed enthusiasm he returned to the chimney. He lowered the pipe once more and tried to fit the loop of rope around the pigeon. Twice he was too slow and the bird passed through the rope before he had time to close the noose. The second time he felt and heard the swish of the bird's stiff tail feathers passing through the rope as it closed around them.

Adam Elston

He tried to stay calm and ignore the sting of sweat that was trickling into his eyes. With great concentration he attempted to fit the loop around the bird once more. Finally, the pigeon lifted one foot and then the other and Patrick saw that the rope had encircled its breast and wings. He held his breath and with his right hand, carefully pulled the loose ends tight. His whole body was tense as he drew the pipe out of the chimney. He could feel the dull weight of the bird and the fragility of its body caught in the noose. When the bird was clear of the lip of the chimney, he raised the pipe above his head. With his right hand he released the pressure on the rope. He watched with exhilaration as the bird swooped away from him. It settled on the crest of a roof a few doors down and then was off again in the direction of the park.

He threw down the pipe and rope onto the flat roof. The lack of any witness to the rescue gave him a sense of anticlimax as he made his way back down into the flat. The room was dim and cool, but when his eyes adjusted to the light he saw shopping bags on the work surface and Helen's purse and keys on the table. He called out her name but she did not reply. He called again and she emerged from the bedroom and he immediately began to tell her about the pigeon. 'I saved the bird, it's gone, I ...' He saw that she had been crying. Such was her apparent strength of character that displays of vulnerability were rare, and all the more unsettling when they did occur.

'What happened?' he asked. 'Are you alright, what is it?'

She came to him and sobbed against his shoulder and he stroked her pale hair. After a moment she sniffed and wiped her eyes with a sleeve as she drew away.

'What is it?' he asked again, more quietly.

She took a shuddering breath and composed herself. 'I've done a test,' she said, 'we're going to have a baby'. She searched his eyes for a reaction. There was none.

Still in the ward, gazing out of the window through the rain, Patrick thought about how the hospital had come to be. He had watched it rise from the ground in stages, and then one day it was finished, as if it had always been there. He thought it must be like the way a tree grows, so slowly that it might not be happening at all. He turned from the window and walked over to where Helen lay with their child, not yet named, in her arms. He bent to kiss her softly on the lips. She smiled, and closed her eyes to receive the kiss.

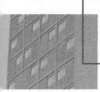

Andrew Lloyd-Jones

Why I Feel Sorry for the Chickens

While I was working at Bradley and Sons, thermometer and pressure gauge manufacturers, they talked about three things. The first was the time the Duke of York made an official visit to the factory in 1995. The second was the Christmas bonus of two frozen chickens each employee had received the previous year and that they were still talking about four months later. The third was Hashkid's trolley dash.

Strictly speaking, Hashkid's trolley dash wasn't really anything to do with the factory, since it happened at Morrisons and not Bradley and Sons, not to mention that it happened on a Saturday. But we all knew Hashkid from work and pretty much everyone we knew from work went to see him do his dash, so I suppose it still counts. Anyway, it's a better story than the time the Duke of York wandered about the factory pretending to be interested in thermometers, and it's infinitely more interesting than two frozen chickens.

I had taken the job when my usual freelance illustration contracts ran dry. For some reason, at the beginning of that year no one was interested in cartoons and, since cartoons is pretty much all I do, I was a bit stuffed otherwise. They made all sorts of different thermometers at Bradley's, from the standard stick-it-in-your-mouth mercury variety to specially designed scientific instruments for measuring the temperature on the moon or whatever. We didn't see much of the interesting ones though, and spent most of our time packing the regular type, which made up the bulk of the business.

My section did the bubble-wrapping. There were myself, Phil, Dan, Emma, Rachel, and Hashkid, all of us linked by our common desire to leave as soon as we could, all of us between jobs for one reason or another. There were also Barbara and Ellen, two women in their fifties. They had been there for as long as anyone could remember and seemed quite happy about it. They were the ones who usually brought up the whole chicken Christmas bonus thing, and at least once a day.

The times we weren't talking about visiting royals or frozen poultry were mostly spent discussing whatever had been on telly the previous night, or rather, Phil would tell us what he'd watched and we'd be invited to comment on his choice of viewing. So when Hashkid came in one day to tell us he'd won a five-minute trolley dash, we were naturally all excited to have something new to talk about.

'DVDs,' said Phil. 'And booze. It's obvious.'

We all nodded.

'Brilliant,' Dan said. 'We'll have a party. Stock up.'

But Hashkid shook his head. 'Thought of that,' he said. 'But you can't. No cigarettes, tobacco, alcohol or non-grocery items, it says.'

'Bollocks,' said Phil. 'That's bollocks.'

We snapped bubble-wrap as we tried to work out what the best things to grab would be.

Hashkid, whose real name was Darren, was so called for his tendency to nip round the back of the factory at lunchtime for what he called a "livener". He had won the trolley dash as part of what he in turn called his "competition strategy". This largely meant entering as many competitions as possible by taking advantage of the no-purchase-necessary rule you see on the back of most of the packs.

'All you have to do for most of them is send in a postcard,' he told me once. 'Once you've got the address of where to send it, it's a piece of piss.'

The addresses came from a magazine he subscribed to called *Win Big!* Every month, it published details of competitions, prizes, and addresses to send the postcards to. The magazine was divided into different sections depending on the type of competition you wanted to enter. Some were simply postcards you had to send off, others involved answering a question or two, still others required you to fill out a crossword puzzle or a word search. But again, Hashkid had it all worked out.

'A lot of people enter everything,' he had told me, 'but I only enter for good stuff. You know, money and cars and that.'

That Hashkid was clearly no fool.

The only reason he'd won the trolley dash, he admitted, was because he'd entered the wrong competition. Instead of the *GQ* BMW draw, he had somehow sent the card to the *Take A Break* Supermarket Bet.

At first, he'd felt sickened, not so much at the embarrassment of such a crap prize, but because, in his mind, he'd been destined to win with that postcard. Had it gone to *GQ*, he told us several times, by now he'd be sitting in a brand-new BMW M3 convertible, probably surrounded by models. Eventually, he got over it, probably because deep down he knew that even though it wasn't the Beemer, and it wasn't a holiday, and it wasn't money, it was still the only thing he'd ever actually won.

'I've broken the dry patch,' he told us. 'It all kicks off from here.'

'Olive oil,' said Rachel eventually.

'Balsamic vinegar,' said Emma.

'Cheese,' said Dan.

'Cheese?' said Phil. 'What are you on about, cheese?'

'Some cheese is quite pricey, actually,' replied Dan. 'Parmesan. French stuff.'

Dan had gone to Durham.

'Bollocks to that,' said Phil. 'In any case, it wouldn't last long enough. Perishable, isn't it?'

'Chocolate,' I suggested.

'Chicken,' said Barbara.

'Shampoo.'

'Moisturiser.'

'Quails' eggs.'

We all looked at Dan again.

'What?' he said. 'They cost a fortune.'

'It's Morrisons, you twat, not Harrods,' said Phil.

'Razor blades.'

This was a tricky one. There followed a discussion as to whether the little cards you pick up in place of the actual razor blades would be honoured for the product they represented, or whether you'd simply end up with a stack of branded cards. It was decided in the end that it was best not to take the risk.

The discussion continued on into the pub after work.

'Smoked salmon.'

'Washing tablets.'

'Batteries.'

'Vitamins.'

'Tampax.'

'They're not expensive,' said Hashkid.

'They are,' said Emma.

Rachel nodded in agreement.

'In any case, it doesn't matter,' said Phil. 'He's not picking out a shitload of tampons.'

'He can do what he likes,' said Emma.

'Water filters.'

'Hair tong gas cartridges.'

'Vitamins.'

'You said that.'

'Suntan lotion.'

'Ribena.'

The night continued like this for a while, every now and again interrupted by an argument as to the value of a potential inclusion.

In the end, the top ten items on the shopping list went as follows, in order of priority:

Batteries

Condoms

Smoked salmon

Parma ham

Washing tablets

Olive oil in fancy bottles

Camera film

Chocolate

Anything organic

Toothbrushes

There were still areas of contention, Rachel and Emma in particular objecting to the lack of feminine hygiene products, but it was generally agreed that this was a fairly good hit list, as long as he could clear the shelves of each item.

'Nice one,' said Phil. 'I reckon you'll get at least a few hundred quid's worth with that lot.'

And so the next Saturday, we all went down to watch Hashkid do his trolley dash. There were a fair number of people there. As well as a group from Morrisons, staff and management and what not, there were photographers from *Take A Break* and the local newspapers, plus a dozen or so customers who had turned up to shop that morning, most of them pensioners.

Hashkid was nervous. You'd have thought he was about to step into the ring. He was jumping up and down, taking deep breaths, shaking his legs out. We all gave him bits of extra advice.

'Make sure your trolley hasn't got a wonky wheel,' Dan said.

'Don't bother with anything on the top or bottom shelves,' I said.

'Use your jumper as a bucket,' said Rachel.

'Don't forget: batteries, condoms, salmon,' said Phil.

'Get us some Tampax, Hash,' said Emma.

'Shut up,' said Phil, 'you'll put him off.'

Hashkid was nodding, flexing his fingers, staring into the aisles ahead of him. This was his defining moment. Morrisons was his Moby Dick.

'I'm okay,' said Hashkid. 'I'm cool.'

We all said good luck and stood back as he posed for photos with the manager of Morrisons and some of the checkout girls.

The manager then stood up and gave a little speech, congratulating Hashkid on winning the competition, and thanking everyone who had turned up. Next they wheeled over the trolley, which looked in good enough condition, and had been decorated with *Take A Break* logos.

Then we all counted down from ten, the manager blew a whistle, and the flashes went as the cameras clicked.

But Hashkid didn't move.

He just stood there, frozen to the spot, with his trolley in front of him, staring straight ahead. There were a couple of seconds of silence, then everyone started yelling, 'Go! Go! Go!' and at last he gave a little jump and raced forwards.

'What was the stupid twat doing?' said Phil as everybody cheered.

'I think he panicked,' said Rachel.

'He's lost at least a minute,' said Phil.

We only caught sight of Hashkid a couple of times after that as he raced about the supermarket.

'He's forgotten the batteries,' Phil said. 'Look, they're right up the front. What's he playing at?'

'He's probably loading up with all the other stuff,' Dan said. 'He'll be fine.'

When it got nearer the time, the manager shouted to the crowd. First one minute, then thirty seconds. Finally we all counted down from ten and Hashkid appeared from one of the aisles with his trolley.

The photographers moved in immediately, and the Morrisons staff held everyone back near the start while they ran his purchases through one of the tills.

'I bloody hope he got the smoked salmon,' said Phil. 'He obviously missed the batteries.'

Suddenly the man holding us all back got a signal from one of the other Morrisons people and moved towards the till. We followed him, pushing through the crowd. People in front of us were laughing as we moved past. Hashkid was standing next to one of the checkouts, looking very pale.

We looked first at Hashkid, and then at what he had grabbed.

In front of him on the belt and now being loaded into about a dozen Morrisons plastic bags were several hundred boxes of tampons, panty liners and feminine wipes. Tampax, Kotex, Always, Bodyform, Alldays – you name it, he'd picked it up. If he'd been playing Feminine Hygiene Bingo, he'd have had the house.

The photographers were pissing themselves as they took shots. They could barely hold their cameras steady. Even the Morrisons manager couldn't keep a straight face. The woman from *Take A Break* on the other hand was nearly as pale as Hashkid. This was clearly going to be difficult to cover in the pages of Britain's Favourite True Life Weekly. Amidst all the stories of abandoned babies, mistaken identities, and heart-warming reunions, a trolley dash by a twenty-five-year-old stoner resulting in a year's worth of tampons wasn't going to play well.

'I don't know what happened,' Hashkid said. 'My mind went blank. All I could think about was tampons.'

'You are having a laugh,' said Phil.

'Did you get anything else?' I said.

'What about the smoked salmon?' said Dan.

Hashkid wasn't even listening to us.

'I couldn't think about anything else,' he was saying. 'This vision of a big vagina popped into my head at the start of the race. I kept seeing that illustration in the little leaflet with the woman, you know, inserting it.'

He spread two of his fingers to demonstrate.

'For fuck's sake, Hash,' I said.

Phil was shaking his head. 'This is your fault,' he said, looking at Emma.

'Why is it my fault?' Emma said.

'Because he never would have even bloody thought about the fucking Tampax if you hadn't mentioned it.'

The picture appeared in the local paper on Monday, and we all read the article over our bubble-wrapped thermometers. Hashkid, undergoing re-entry at about two thousand degrees, looking miserable. The manager, a breezy room temperature, just about keeping it together. The woman from *Take A Break*, frozen to the spot, mortified, several degrees below zero. Half a dozen Morrisons staff in various degrees of laughter.

The headline read: *On The Rag, Get Set, Go!* We photocopied the article and put it up all over the warehouse.

Hashkid obviously had to put up with a lot of jokes for a while after that. Even Barbara and Ellen stopped talking about the chickens for a few days. He cancelled his subscription to *Win Big!* and ended up giving the tampons and stuff away. He put the whole lot in a big box in the factory with a sign saying 'Help yourself' above it. I never saw any of them being taken, but by the end of the summer they were nearly all gone.

By that stage I'd found enough freelance work to keep me going, and so I handed in my notice. Hashkid had left a month earlier, as had Phil, Dan and Rachel. There was only me and Emma left from the group I'd started with, not including Barbara and Ellen. Emma and I kept in touch and went out a few times after that, but it wasn't really happening and we sort of let it go.

I spoke to Phil though the other day. He'd got his job at the factory through an aunt who was still working there. She told him that Barbara had won a round-the-world trip with spending money and had taken a month off to travel. Apparently she'd entered a competition on the back of a box of feminine wipes.

She took Ellen with her. So I imagine they've got something new to talk about now.

But, personally, I feel sorry for the chickens.

Guy
Ware

Cities from a train

For Victor, the end began when he read in a local paper the story of a man who had attempted – and failed – to run a marathon backwards. The runner had been trying to raise funds for research into a rare neurological disease, which causes sufferers gradually to regress, unlearning step by step all the skills they have amassed during their lifetime. Unlike more common forms of dementia, it is not memories that are lost but the ability to reason and to interpret them, along with the acquired motor skills, making it progressively more difficult to function effectively, then independently, then finally to walk or stand at all until the victim is left mewling and puking like an infant. At this point the disease appears to resolve itself spontaneously, allowing or requiring the patient to begin all over again the business of life, to relearn the physical and theoretical skills needed to make sense of the innumerable memories still crowding his or her brain. Confronted by the enormity, the terror and – Victor imagined – the futility of the task, the majority of patients become depressed or delusional, and recovery is rarely complete.

He had found the paper on his seat. It was a local freesheet from a small city though which his train would pass, but which he believed he had never visited. At first, he had simply moved it to the vacant place next to his in the hope that it might discourage anyone else from sitting there.

He had not been on a train – a proper train, he thought, with toilets and a buffet car, a train that carved through fields, leaving one town before it reached the next instead of merely halting from suburb to suburb as if following a string of sausages – for as long as he could remember. This one had seemed familiar enough, though: crowded, cramped, his seat comfortable but facing backwards – his back to the engine – a little plastic tray folding down into his lap from the rear of the seat in front. Or the front of the seat behind, he supposed, from the train's point of view, or from that of an observer on the platform, had there been anyone to watch him leave. He had balanced a paper coffee cup on the tray, then had to grab it quickly when the child taking possession of the seat in front – he'd say in front for simplicity, he thought: a child of ten or so, older than Lily, anyway – started to experiment with the recline button.

When the train pulled out, on time, Victor had watched the metropolis slide backwards out of view. He had travelled back, like the angel of history, watching through glass as the wreckage piled up behind him, propelling him full-tilt before an ever-burgeoning past.

All this was familiar.

There was something wrong, however; or something not quite right, at least. It tugged at Victor, abrading his nerves. He tried to skewer the source of his unease, but could not, and turned to the abandoned newspaper for distraction. Then, approaching a satellite town, the train rattled across the points and Victor was jolted into recognising that the problem was not a carcass he could lay out on the block, but an absence, a hole where something should have been. The train's constant, sucking sibilation had not been punctuated by the clicking of the rails; there had been none of the diggety-dig, diggety-dig that had characterised all trains in the stories he had told Lily every day for what now seemed a lifetime. Another lifetime. It was progress, he supposed; but without that rhythmic clatter he thought he'd find it harder to attain the hypnotic suspension that he had always thought of as the main benefit of a lengthy train journey. To travel vacantly was, to Victor's mind, a better thing than to arrive.

Certainly better than to arrive today. He pictured his sister waiting for him at the station: a study of rude, bovine health, her over-large hands skulking in her armpits or beating each other for warmth, the woollen flaps of her inane Tibetan hat jogging like the ears of an excited spaniel as she stomped forward to crush him to her solid, creaturely udders and over-larded ribs. She'd make some comment about how he seemed to have lost weight, how there was nothing to him now; it was as if his mother hadn't died at all, but had simply stolen the body of her daughter. Victor would wonder what they had done with the real Freddie, if perhaps somewhere there was a slim, happy but less boisterous and impressionable young woman who had grown from the awkward, clever adolescent he remembered.

She'd drive him home, to the house, in a battered, anonymous car that she'd have attempted to endow with personality by granting it a name culled from children's books or television, or from her half-baked readings of Chinese philosophy, which name he would be invited to guess from the discomforts of the car or the alarming noises it emitted. She'd refuse to be put off by his obtuse responses – Myra, after Hindley, perhaps? Or: Victor? you named it after me? Hirohito? – until at last she'd laugh and slap him on the shoulder and say something like, no, silly, it's *Muttley*. Didn't you hear that chugging laugh when I started him up? Isn't that perfect? And then, at that moment, he would remember that Freddie had christened a previous car Violet Elizabeth on account of the tooth-shattering scream it let out whenever she engaged second gear. And he would agree that, yes, it was perfect. They'd be silent for a while, listening to the noise of the engine, and then she would turn to look at him and say something like, But seriously, Victor, how have you been?

And he'd say something non-committal, like, Oh, you know.

And she'd say, Yeah, I guess we never knew how much we took her for granted until she was gone. How much we loved her.

And he'd think, but would not say: Speak for yourself.

Then they would arrive and his father would be in the wrong half of the house for the first time in – what? – twenty-five years? He'd be in her half, downstairs, in the living room – his mother's bedroom – playing the paterfamilias, welcoming relatives and pointing them towards the flimsy reed coffin parked squarely on the bed, or towards the table where there'd be cans of lager and glasses of sherry and peanuts still in their foil packets for later, for the guests, the mourners, to help themselves, he'd say, when they came back afterwards. His father would nod and ask how he was, perhaps even ask how Sara was, and the little one. He wouldn't remember his granddaughter's name, but then Victor would stop to wonder whether he had, in fact, ever told him it was Lily, and would think there didn't seem to be much point now.

His father would introduce him to the man from the Humanist Society he'd found on the Internet, who was going to do the oration. The humanist man would never have met Victor's mother, who'd been a Catholic, attending Mass and regularly confessing whatever middling sins she had managed to accumulate: mostly anger, Victor supposed. She had christened neither of her children, thanks to their father's objections, but she had cooked fish every Friday. She had left some on the stairs for Victor's father to take up and eat in his half of the house, alone, and had done so even after he'd announced through Freddie that he had become a vegetarian. He had declared his vegetarianism, Victor now recalled, at about the time that he himself had decided to become a butcher. Or perhaps it was the other way around? Freddie, the diplomat, had described for them both the famous (she said) Taoist figure of the butcher who had carved oxen with the grace of a dancer. The point was not *what* one did, she said, but *how* one approached the task; provided that one brought no extrinsic purpose to it, then any action could be right, she said. Neither Victor nor his father had been convinced.

Victor would shake hands with a sprinkling of distant, dimly remembered relatives and would be unable to recall the last time they had met. He would try to evade their polite questions about Sara (and/or the little one) or about life in the metropolis, about business, about the shop. He would fail to ask them any questions in return, and the conversations would expire gracelessly, like fish stranded in mud as the floodwaters recede.

There would be no line of beetle-black Daimlers blocking the narrow road outside the house. No: they would drive out to a freezing, wind-whipped hillside in a haphazard congeries of vehicles, Victor once again beside his sister in Muttley, their mother in the back of their father's van, boxed up for delivery to her last, inevitable indignity. Perhaps in another lifetime the cemetery might grow to fit its sylvan promise of a woodland burial; but for now, Victor foresaw, it would remind him of nothing so much as archive footage from the First World War, the sky dark and wet, the ground ripped open to black mud, through which they would pass with jerky, unnatural movements and false consolation, all sound sucked away.

He knew none of this, of course: it was mere supposition, predicated on the wreckage of past experience.

He did not know exactly how his father would seek the final say in the violent, soundless war that had been going on for maybe three decades, but he knew the opportunity would not be missed. He foresaw that he would be forced somehow to participate in a final act of degradation that would demean them all. For once, his father would wield without mediation the power to impose himself, to make his mark; it would be childish of Victor to suppose that he might exercise restraint. After all, Victor asked himself, would he? When the time came, would he act any differently?

Only when the train pulled out of a station did Victor realise that it had even stopped. He watched the unknown city recede as they beat through fields of lumpy, fibrous vegetables that gave off the odour of wet towels. As the train gathered speed, he returned to the paper and found that it was local to the city they had just left. It was not a place he had ever visited, he thought, or probably ever would, but he supposed it might contain its own share of misery and absurdity: the story of the marathon runner's perverse and ill-fated attempt to ameliorate the impact of his father's degenerative brain disease seemed promising.

It had evidently been a slow news week; the journalist had been afforded ample space to provide colour and detail. The onset of the disease is gradual, Victor read, but it usually accelerates dramatically as the sufferer re-approaches those stages of life when he or she had learned the most. The runner's father, for example – a retired master butcher whose shop was treasured in the town, but which the runner had not chosen to take over – had at first noticed only that his golf was deteriorating, the slice he'd finally cured after retirement returning to send balls flying into the lake at the sixth. Then one Sunday, carving a perfect rib joint, he had noticed that, while he knew his son was a great disappointment to him, he could no longer work out why. Later, Victor read, the same had become true of his wife who, some years earlier, had died of Creutzfeldt-Jakob Disease for reasons the butcher could no longer bring to mind. After a while, however, his family ceased to disappoint him altogether and became, momentarily, a source of intense satisfaction, even joy.

There followed a brief but traumatic period during which the butcher lost all knowledge of cuts and cooking times and hanging periods, and of the use and maintenance of knives. Knowing they were sharp, would slice meat and should be handled with care did not prevent him cutting the tip off his tongue while eating pasta with a boning knife. He lost the thumb and two fingers of his left hand attempting with a cleaver to turn his granddaughter's pet rabbits into sausages. (As he read this, the scars on Victor's own hands seemed to throb.) In hospital the scale of the butcher's problems became apparent and diagnosis possible at about the same time as his ability to understand the implications disappeared forever.

The runner was described as an athlete, a vegetarian and a former life coach. He had run for eleven hours fifty-six before collapsing in agony at the twenty-second mile. Victor smiled. The runner's wife was said to be very proud of what he had done for his father, although the resulting damage to both Achilles tendons was certain to affect his future performance, his career and sponsorship potential, and so to threaten the security of their young family.

Victor told Freddie about the story as they crawled out of the station in *Wu-wei* (named, she explained, after the Taoist slogan of 'non-purposive action', which, she felt, described perfectly the car's un-businesslike approach to the business of transportation). In response, she said what a coincidence that was. They'd been there, to that city, as children: did he remember?

Victor didn't.

Their father had taken them on a mystery trip, Freddie said, back when he was still speaking to mum. They'd all gone to the bus station and taken the first coach that left: that was where they'd ended up.

Victor remembered the trip but said it was to somewhere else, that their mother hadn't come because it had been a Sunday morning.

He wanted Freddie to be wrong. He wanted her to talk about the former life coach. He wanted to tease her, to ask if one could retrospectively improve one's past lives, thereby exponentially enhancing the quality of the karma one brought to one's present incarnation? He wanted Freddie solemnly to point out the dangers of such karmic time travel, to fret about its unpredictable consequences, about the possibility that the coach's client might suddenly cease to exist or be spontaneously recreated elsewhere, heedlessly disrupting the lives of the family and friends of his new identity. He wanted her to worry that the previous holder of that identity might be consigned to non-existence or recreation in another, perhaps lower form. He wanted her to ask how Victor would feel, for instance, if he were suddenly required to metamorphose into a cockroach so that a previously under-evolved being could take over his life with Sara and Lily?

Then Victor would say he knew exactly how that felt.

Freddie would turn to look at him, but he'd say no more, and she'd have to turn back to watch the road.

That was what he wanted, but it wasn't going to happen now.

They pulled up outside the house. Freddie said: 'Go easy on Dad, Victor. You might find he's acting a little ... strange.'

Victor snorted. 'No change there, then.'

'Really. Despite everything, he's taken this very hard.'

'So hard he's got to bury her under a tree?'

'What?'

'With a few feeble mumblings from a total stranger?'

Freddie looked at Victor for a long time. 'What's happened, Victor? Has something happened with Sara?'

'Oh, you know,' said Victor.

Freddie didn't and Victor didn't say. Eventually she gave up.

'You'll be nice to Father Calley, too, won't you?'

Victor was surprised. 'Will he even be there?'

'I should think so,' said Freddie. 'He's saying the Mass.'

The churchyard was cold, but sheltered from the wind. Afterwards, during the wake, which was large and, for the most part, good-humoured, Victor asked Freddie to drive him back to the station.

'What are you going to do?' she said. 'When you get home?'

'I'm not going home.'

'Then where?'

'There's a place, a city. About halfway back from here. I told you about it this morning. There'll be an opening for a good butcher there.'

Freddie smiled, and they embraced. 'Take care,' she said.

Victor held up both hands, palms outwards, fingertips spread. There were more scars than he could remember, but all ten digits remained. 'I always have,' he said.

Nicholas Royle

Bus Spotting

I phoned Cathy from King's Cross, and again from Euston Square. I'd have phoned her from all the way round the Circle Line if I'd thought it would make any difference. I asked her if she would keep an open mind until I got back to Manchester and we had a chance to talk, face to face.

Cathy had dumped me. She had 'made some changes in her life'. She'd done it on the phone, which served me right in a way, seeing as how I'd finished with Sally Sullivan on the phone six months earlier so I could go out with Cathy. Gorgeous, buxom Sally from Buxton. No one had ever kissed like her, nor ever would again. It was odd that I thought myself honourable enough to finish with Sally before asking Cathy out, but hadn't had the decency to meet Sally to tell her in person. I suppose, when you're eighteen, Buxton seems like a bit of a trek from Altrincham, just to tell someone it's over. I'd never even been to see her in Buxton anyway, despite the fact she had her own flat there (she was five years my senior). We always met in town and went to places like Pips, Legend, Rafters. We saw the Psychedelic Furs at Rotters and Fad Gadget at the Squat supported by Performance. At another Fad Gadget gig at Eden we saw Bernard Albrecht, as he called himself then, and Peter Hook, and I asked them for their autographs. I asked Hooky to sign twice and he snarled: 'Trying to make yourself a fucking millionaire?' But he signed twice anyway. Vain bastard.

Life got its own back on me. Cathy dumped me, as I say, on the blower. We didn't have email then, or mobiles & fckng txt msgs. Otherwise I'm sure she would have shielded herself as much as she could. As soon as I hung up I remembered I was in London, in the middle of trying to find a place to live.

College started in three weeks. I'd got no money, no flat-share, no room in halls – and now, suddenly, no girlfriend either. Hence the trip round the Circle Line to Euston and trains back home to Manchester. I still do call it home even though my folks, the moment I boarded the train for London, sold our old house and moved up north to the Lakes.

Iggy had said he would meet me. Iggy was my best mate. Iggy wasn't his real name. If I'd ever been told his real name, I'd forgotten it. Iggy was a shortarse bastard like me and spectacularly untidy. He wore a cancer-shop jacket with a packet of Marlboro sticking out the top pocket, and although he hardly ever looked at you when he was talking to you and he never introduced you unless you said who the fuck's this person talking to us, I liked him a lot. I never understood why he made a point of wearing odd socks, but then he couldn't get his head round my having been a bus spotter and, at school, a founder member of the Public Service Vehicle Group. We got on.

He met me at Piccadilly in his Ford Escort that was so old and battered it felt more like a prototype than a Mark One. He'd recently had it resprayed – in undercoat. The ashtrays were all full and Iggy had started stubbing out his fags on the dash. I was meant to be staying at Iggy's mum's place in Gatley, but for some reason we both ended up staying at Paz's house in Navigation Road. Anyone who thinks Altrincham is posh wants to stop a night at Paz's. Located at the Broadheath end of Navvy Road, Paz's house redefined squalor. It was a two-up-two-down with scabrous pebble dash like a bad case of psoriasis. It got worse when you went inside. It was a demolition site, not so much hard to let as impossible to donate to Shelter. Paz was its only saving grace, which isn't saying much. His face always looked slept-in, his eyes like two little twinkling diamonds set in a cushion of crinkly paper. He had one of those Shredded Wheat moustaches.

At 4a.m. Iggy and I found ourselves walking along the towpath of the Bridgewater Canal talking about the way things were changing – in our lives rather than down the canal, although it wouldn't be long before they built a new estate bang opposite where we'd fished all through the heatwave of 1976. Tiny little mirror carp, the odd leather; perch and, of course, roach. If you've never fished, you won't know this, but roach are the most boring fish going. Naturally, therefore, they are the most plentiful. And no, they're not boring because they're plentiful; they're boring because they're boring. They don't put up a fight and they never grow bigger than farts, a fart being anything under four ounces.

We didn't get to bed till 6.30a.m., which meant I'd been up twenty-four hours, give or take. I got three hours' sleep before Paz's household began to stir.

I phoned Cathy in the morning and she sounded very down. With Iggy and Tommo, who was also staying at Paz's, we got the 263 into Manchester to eat at one of the Indian caffs at the back of Tib Street. These were new to me. Previously Tib Street had meant only one thing as far as I was concerned and that was pet shops. Quite possibly there was only ever one pet shop on Tib Street, but in my mind it was lined with the bastards. On both sides. It stank of fur and seeds, and there were feathers everywhere. The tricks that memory plays on you. Just like there were fourteen hundred seedy second-hand bookshops on Shude Hill. And that weird bloke with the obscenely dark, luscious triangular beard worked in all of them. To Iggy, Tib Street meant cheap curry houses. Not far away was Stevenson Square, where Maynes Buses ran from; apparently the man who owned Maynes Buses was the brother of the Mr Mayne who was an English teacher at our school in Rusholme, which is also renowned for its cheap curry houses. Small world or what?

Iggy, Tommo and Paz got the bus back to Alty, but I was due to meet Cathy at Piccadilly. I was not looking forward to it. I fucking loved this girl. There she was. We kissed. It didn't feel right. We got the train from platform 14 and went back to Paz's. There must have been about seventeen better alternatives but that's what we did. We went upstairs and spent hours talking, crying, pleading, discussing and, after lengthy debate, shagging. We went to the chippy on Manchester Road and shared a bag of chips outside the ice rink.

Iggy took Cathy and me back to Piccadilly. It was strange the three of us being in the same car, because of course Cathy had gone out with Iggy before she went out with me. True, she'd gone out with me for longer, but it was over now for me as well, or so it seemed. I'd find out for certain the following day when I was due to go to Wilmslow for the final session of our summit meeting.

She turned and offered me a sad little smile.

As I watched her train trundle out of Piccadilly, I reckoned I knew what she was going to say the following day. I didn't want to lose her. She was easily the best girlfriend I'd ever had. She might not have been as glamorous as Sally Sullivan, who got dolled up like Marilyn for our nights out in town, but she was exciting in her own way. The way she kissed was amazing – her darting little tongue – and made me go all hot. The way she whispered things in my ear, like someone a lot older, older even than Sally Sullivan, emulsified the bones in my legs. To think that for what seemed like years, but was only a matter of months, I'd had to watch her and Iggy together. I'd always felt I'd noticed her first and had staked my claim by mentioning to Iggy that I fancied her. I remain convinced to this day that it only occurred to him to ask her out after I'd been indiscreet. Iggy was so charming, despite his junk-shop couture, that no matter whom he asked out, they always said yes.

I had my chance when Terry Rhodes – swotty kid, not too popular, glasses, big briefcase – announced on a crowded top deck one afternoon on the way home from school that he'd seen Cathy the week before at a bus stop on Palatine Road with Steve Brabyn and they'd been snogging. Rhodes shook his head as if judging Cathy. We were all on the top deck that day – me, Cathy and Iggy – which was unusual because Iggy normally caught the 45. He was coming back to mine to have a look at – and possibly take the piss out of – my recently acquired complete set of Greater Manchester Passenger Transport Executive bus timetables. Cathy got the 41 to Sale, where her dad picked her up because he worked in Timperley. When Terry Rhodes's megaphoned allegations reached us, Cathy simply denied it.

Rhodes shouted back: 'Yes, you were. I saw you. It was half past five. I saw you. Half past five.'

I hated him, in his nasty, Sellotaped glasses and his big fuck-off briefcase full of Latin books. What business was it of his? The chiselling nosy bastard.

Cathy retorted that she'd got as far as Sale by 5.30. She knew because she got the 41X to Woodheys, she said, and when she got off the newsagent's was still open and it always shut at 5.30 and – turning to Iggy – Iggy could check that if he didn't believe her.

He said he believed her.

I bit my lip.

On the Monday, I got a 264 into Manchester, walked from Deansgate up to Piccadilly, and got the train to Wilmslow. During the summer when we still lived in Alty, I'd always cycled to Wilmslow down the A538, often stopping halfway and fishing for crucian carp in a tiny little pit next to one of the runways at Manchester Airport. Very few people knew about the crucian pit.

Our window-cleaner – Jim, lived on Colwick Avenue, made his own floats – told me about it. Maybe he only told me about it because we had some pampas grass growing in our front garden on Ellesmere Road, and pampas grass, I was to discover, was very good for making floats with. I let Jim have some pampas grass and he told me about the crucian pit. I recognised the passing on of this knowledge as an important rite. The location of the pit was secret lore known only to a very few, and now I was among the select. I told Iggy about it and he came and fished it with me, the two of us pelting down the A538 on our bikes, enormous wicker fishing baskets strapped to the racks, great big rod bags rattling over our shoulders.

Two hundred yards before the road went under the runway you stopped and carried your bike up the steep embankment. We fought our way through the hawthorn hedge and left our bikes in the first field, then ducked under the fence on the other side and navigated a safe route through the waist-high nettles around the pit. You came upon it so suddenly it was amazing no one ever fell in.

It was the most beautiful and magical location of my adolescence, and it was always difficult cycling past it to get to Wilmslow, even when I knew Cathy was waiting for me at the other end.

I walked from the railway station to Stockton Road. Cathy opened the door a crack, let me in. We stood in each other's arms for a minute and I felt her shaking and I knew that she had made her decision.

We walked down to the golf course and I sat on the stile. We said nothing for a long time – there was no need. Then she was saying she was sorry. 'I love her,' I'd written in my diary, which normally recorded my catch at the canal or the crucian pit. 'I bloody love her.' We walked to the cricket ground where we sat on a bench. Later we walked back to the station, where we said goodbye.

In Manchester it hit me. I phoned her and asked her to reconsider. I begged her to see me again before I went back to London, but she said she couldn't because she'd promised to see a friend.

The next morning, Iggy, Tommo, Paz and I drove up to Worsley Woods in Iggy's car and went mushroom-picking. We didn't look in the actual woods, but in cows' fields near them. Iggy told me to look very carefully, especially near cow pats. I was told to look out for the familiar dark brown nipple. We picked eighty mushrooms and took them back to Paz's where they were laid out to dry.

In the afternoon I sat on the swings in John Leigh Park, looked in the second-hand bookshop on Regent Street, and tried calling Cathy, but there was no answer. I don't know if they'd invented the answering machine in 1982, but Cathy's parents certainly didn't have one.

Back at Paz's, I was sceptical and nervous. But, I reasoned, one of the worst things that could happen had actually happened, and I was safe(ish) among friends. How much worse could things get? I found Paz and Tommo a bit intimidating because they were a few years older than me and each lived in a tip. I'd never seen Tommo's place, but by all accounts he made Paz seem like the Howard Hughes of south Manchester. As for Paz, he had a habit, according to Iggy, of masturbating in every room of his house, including houses he stayed in or visited, and even in his car, including once while he was driving it over to Leeds on the M62.

Tommo was possibly the scariest. There was something wild about Tommo that you could see in his eyes. It was as if he was aware that he wouldn't live for very long, so he was determined to be as dirty and as wicked as possible in what little time he'd got left.

Shortly after meeting Tommo for the first time, I was fishing on my own at King George's at the back of the bus depot in Alty. I was up by the pipe, a swim where you either got loads of bites or nothing at all, and it was getting difficult to see my float in the dusk. I did a circuit of the pool to see if there was a free swim with more potential and better light. I came across Tommo with two others in the corner swim by the gate, where I would never consider fishing, just as you'd never be entirely happy sitting by the door in a restaurant.

'Hiya,' I said, shyly.

Tommo looked at me from under his blond fringe, the corners of his mouth turned down in what passed for a smile in Tommo's world, his eyes all bloodshot, and gave a sort of snuffly chuckle.

''ad owt?' I asked him.

He looked at his two mates who both twitched their rod-tips.

'Few farts,' he said with another laugh.

They'd put their keepnets out, though. I didn't ask to see inside them. Tommo told me later that all three nets were full almost to the point of swimming away – packed with tench, silver bream, crucians and roach.

Nothing under a pound and a half. Even the roach.

I was always in awe of Iggy for having this relationship with Paz and Tommo. Also because he smoked twenty a day, drove his own car, and had a girlfriend who wasn't planning on ditching him when he went off to Oxford.

Poly.

Plus, he knew how to recognise magic mushrooms.

We had the mushrooms in a pot of tea, eighty of them between four of us. There was a distinctive taste to the tea, but it wasn't unpleasant. Collective anticipation created a tense atmosphere in the house and it was less than half an hour before the first one went. I forget who it was, but he went in fits of uncontrollable giggles that were so infectious the other two joined in even before their mushrooms had taken effect. I remained sceptical. I couldn't believe that a hatful of shit-eating mushrooms freely available in farmers' fields within walking distance of a million Mancs could possibly have any kind of effect.

As the others gradually yielded to collective hysteria, I began to feel slightly out of it and to give myself something to do I picked up Paz's headphones and chose something to listen to from his record collection. I'd never heard Vangelis's 'Spiral' before. It was something else. So much so that after a few minutes of its drilling through my head I started seeing little pictures on top of the television set. Bright little neon figures and cartoon shapes trooping across the top of the box. A parade of swans dancing in time to the music.

I took the headphones off as I realised that I'd started giggling in sporadic bursts. Nothing further happened for a while, although the other lads were all pretty much off their heads by now. I changed the record to an LP by Gong, 'Camembert Electrique' – 'From the Planet Gong' it said on the sleeve – and within seconds of getting into a track called 'Mister Long Shanks: O Mother I Am Your Fantasy' I was halfway to Planet Gong myself. Always a soft touch for breathy, ethereal female vocals, I realised I'd stumbled upon one of the most significant songs of my life.

I was gone now, completely gone. I joined the others in the kitchen, where they were crouching on the floor gazing in wondrous adoration at the ceiling. I saw why. The kitchen ceiling was transparent. No, it really was transparent. It was made of that see-through corrugated plastic stuff they make verandas with and the effect of the purple sky luminescing through the kitchen ceiling was nothing short of transcendental.

There was a shout from the hall. Paz was at the foot of the stairs pointing upwards in disbelief. 'I can't climb the fucking stairs,' he said. 'The bastard stairs have turned into a fucking cliff face.' And then he fell over.

The thing was, he was right. Maybe it was a trick of the light – and a trick of the 'shrooms – but the steps appeared to have been ironed flat. We tried to climb them but we just slid down in fits of hysterical laughter.

I don't know who it was suggested we go out, but within minutes we were walking up Hawarden Road, left into Ellesmere Road, past our old house, up Hazel Road, and before long we were heading down Oakfield Street towards the bus depot. Tommo wandered up someone's front path to have a really close look at the stone cladding. 'Look at that fucking texture,' he crooned as we dragged him away.

In those days you could still get into the depot at times when there was no one around, such as in the middle of the night. We headed round the side of the shed, where a few big hulking Leylands loomed by the entrance, and entered the yard at the back. There was a wire-mesh fence, but it was a bit pointless when you could just stroll in from the street.

This was in pre-deregulation days, so all the buses were still orange, even at night as there was enough low-level lighting from the swimming pool car park. A brand-new Foden double-decker gleamed like an enormous toy just taken out of its box. There were a couple of those stumpy little Centreline things that ran between Piccadilly and Victoria, although there was no good reason for them to be sleeping it off at Altrincham since the code PS told you they were both based at Princess Road. A handful of old single-deckers still carried the SELNEC logo; allocated to ST – Stockport – they, too, were interlopers here. Right at the back of the yard in regal isolation sat a dark green colossus. Silently we approached it – a withdrawn Crosville monster with rear concertina doors.

Paz worked the emergency door mechanism and we climbed on board. The rows of empty seats were lined up like dominoes stood on their edges. Push one over and they'd all go. Tommo was trying to climb the stairs and finding it as difficult as we had back at Paz's. We made it eventually and all collapsed on double seats, spaced out on the top deck. Mostly we just gazed at whatever we found in front of our faces: the ceiling with its lovely rounded cornices and recessed light bulbs; the crimson ceramic bell-push; the shiny chrome rails on the backs of the seats. Occasionally we exclaimed that something was 'bazzing' or 'dobbing' or 'fucking ace'.

Iggy came and sat in the seat behind mine and leaned over, grinning at me.

'You're a jousey bastard, you are,' I said.

'Why's that?'

'You know. You've got a girlfriend and she wouldn't finish with you just because you moved away.'

'She might,' he said. 'Anything could happen.'

Iggy and his girlfriend were going to different polys. These were nervous times for all of us. Or at least for me and Iggy. Paz and Tommo weren't going anywhere, apart from fishing down at George's and, in Paz's case, pulling off in other people's bedrooms.

'She was never reliable,' I said. 'Cathy.'

'No?'

'No. Remember that time she swore blind she was on the 41X and when she got off at Woodheys the newsagent's was still open? That was how she knew it was before half past five, because that shop always closed at half five? So she couldn't have been necking with Steve Brabyn at a bus stop on Palatine Road like Terry Rhodes said she was?'

Iggy nodded.

'Well, the 41X doesn't go to Woodheys, does it? It terminates at Sale Vine. It's the 41 that goes all the way to Woodheys. She was lying. She was snogging Steve Brabyn at a bus stop on Palatine Road. When she was supposed to be going out with you.'

I felt a certain small and slightly pathetic sense of triumph as a dark look fell across Iggy's face.

'I know that,' he said after a moment. 'Do you think I don't know that?'

The next day I returned to London.

It took a while to get over Cathy. About a term and a half. It wasn't as if all the girls in London were minging, but no one quite matched up to her, and it took me that long to realise they didn't have to. 'Plenty more fish in the sea,' my dad said over the phone. Eventually I met one, a girl from Edgbaston called Liz, and she straightened me out – at least for a while. She took me home to meet her mother who sat me down and offered me a cup of tea. 'Earl Grey or normal?' she asked. 'What the fuck's Earl Grey?' I almost said, just managing not to. 'Earl Grey, please,' I responded, wanting to impress, and Liz's mum brought me a cup of tea brewed with magic mushrooms. Or so I thought as I spluttered my first mouthful onto the magnolia carpet. I'd tasted Earl Grey before, it transpired, but only once, in Paz's house the night I split up with Cathy, and I hadn't known it was called Earl Grey. It hadn't been the mushrooms, I now realised, that had made the tea taste strange. It was the tea.

Iggy and I went back to Worsley Woods a few years later, after we'd both got our qualifications and were wondering what to do next. Iggy had a new car with bigger ashtrays, but his girlfriend was off the scene. Paz and Tommo were thinking about buying a big old house together and doing it up. I wondered about calling Tommo and warning him about Paz's habit, but decided it would be funnier not to. For three months I'd been going out with a wardrobe mistress from a fringe theatre in Marylebone and had no plans to move back up north.

Iggy parked just off Leigh Road, close to the canal. We walked along the towpath. I didn't really know the area, having only visited it once, but Iggy knew it well. He stopped, shook his head regretfully, and pointed.

The field where we'd picked our mushrooms had been ploughed over.

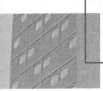

Notes on Contributors

Kate Ansell has escaped West London for the coastal thrills of Brighton, but still holds down a day job somewhere inside the M25. Occasionally she writes features for the BBC's Ouch! website. Sometimes she does short stories. Mostly she is working on a novel.

Jonathan Attrill was born and lives in London. He has worked as a warehouseman, musician, mental health support worker, and basic skills tutor. In 1995 he gained an honours degree in European Cultural History from Middlesex University. He has won the short story category of The London Writers Competition (2004), and also The 'Poetry Monthly' Open Booklet Competition (2005) with his poetry collection *Lateral History*. He now facilitates creative writing for people with mental health difficulties.

Melissa Bellovin, a Long Island native, lives in London. She has written many short stories and is at work on an MFA and a novel about love, teleportation and finding a home. Her most unfortunate characteristic is a short attention span, and her favourite writers died long ago and wrote about whales, street urchins, locked-up maidens, and the anguish and frailty of existence.

Paul Blaney has taught creative writing in Britain and America, and written numerous short stories, one of which was awarded the Tom Gallon prize by the Society of Authors. He has also written three novellas, one set in London, one in Hong Kong during the Handover, and the third on a container ship bound for Lisbon. The themes of his recently completed novel, *Mister Spoonface*, are the fertility industry and 21st-century fatherhood. Paul recently moved from London to New Jersey, from where he continues to help organise Tales of the DeCongested.

Katy Darby divides between writing short stories, plays, and That Difficult Second Novel. She's previously been published by Samuel French (plays) on pulp.net and carvezine.com (short stories), and in the *London Magazine*, the Arvon anthology, and on London buses (poetry and journalism). She lived in King's Cross, London, working in fringe theatres and press offices, until 2005, but is currently in Norwich, on the University of East Anglia's MA in creative writing.

Patricia Debney's first collection of prose poems, *How to Be a Dragonfly* (Smith/Doorstop Books, 2005), won the 2004 Poetry Business Book & Pamphlet competition, and her novella, *Losing You*, is forthcoming from Bluechrome (2007). Her prize-winning short stories have appeared in journals and anthologies, and her libretto for the chamber opera, *The Juniper Tree*, premiered with the London Sinfonietta to critical acclaim. She teaches creative writing at the University of Kent and lives in Canterbury with her composer partner and their two children.

Tadeusz Deręgowski was born in Lusaka, Zambia, in 1969, but was brought up in Scotland where he studied Fine Art at Edinburgh University and Edinburgh College of Art. He then moved to London where he has had several exhibitions of paintings and prints. He has produced illustrations for newspapers and magazines including the *Sunday Telegraph* and *The Spectator*. He has been writing short stories and giving readings for the last four years.

Adam Elston was born in 1972. He is a journalist and lives in North London. He has been writing fiction for three years and is currently working on a collection of short stories.

Sally Foote was born in Cape Town in 1974. She studied journalism and worked as a documentary writer for two years in Johannesburg before relocating to London. She was the winner of the 2005 Time Out short story competition and is working on her first novel.

Frank Goodman won the Wandsworth London Writer competition back in '94 and was the Churchill Theatre's New Playwright of the Year in 2002. To date he has completed one novel, five plays (one of which was performed at the Churchill Theatre, Bromley in July 2006) and innumerable short stories. He is currently putting the finishing touches to a (hopefully) comic novel about a fringe theatre playwright and a writing play about the relationship between Anaïs Nin and Henry Miller.

Lewis Hall was born in Leeds in 1984. Reading *Trash*, at Tales of the DeCongested in 2004, spurred him on to make more submissions and experiment with his writing. In the space of four months in 2005 Lewis graduated from Lancaster University with a BA in 'English Literature with Creative Writing', completed an intensive CELTA (English as a foreign language) teaching course and fled England to teach English in Taiwan.

Sally Hinchcliffe was one of the first students to take the MA in creative writing at Birkbeck, where she helped set up and edit the first issue of *The Mechanics' Institute Review*. Her story 'Gerald Says' was broadcast on Radio 4 in 2005 and 'In Heaven There Is No Beer' will be appearing in the Asham Award Anthology *Don't Know A Good Thing*. She is currently living in London and working on a novel.

Born in West London in 1972, **Sara Hiorns** was brought up in North London and now lives in East London with her husband and daughter. She has written a number of short stories, a biography of her grandmother, and is near to completing a novel that looks at the effects of regeneration (or "gentrification") on areas of London. Sara studied English at Sussex and History at Goldsmiths and has done a great deal of work on London's history. She joined the diplomatic service in 2004.

Born in Warsaw in 1973, **Marek Kazmierski** moved to London as a teenager, and has always been a keen writer and painter. Following years of life research (as a restaurateur, translator, stripper, teacher, security guard, etc.), he now leads a library-based project in Feltham prison. He is also hard at work on a self-penned/directed/acted feature film, *The Fifth Season*, which combines the genres of poetry, prose and cinematic drama (www.songofzen.com).

Rebekah Lattin-Rawstrone was born in Kenya and now lives in Bethnal Green. She has written numerous short stories, one of which won The Promis Prize for Young Writers in The London Writers Award 2002, and is working on her second novel. Her first novel, *Correspondence*, received a Graham Greene Birthplace Trust Award in 2004. She teaches creative writing at City University and co-founded Tales of the DeCongested.

Andrew Lloyd-Jones was born in 1971 and grew up in Anchorage, Alaska. He studied English Literature at the University of York, and currently lives in London. His fiction has been featured on Pulp.Net, in the Canongate anthology *Original Sins*, and in 2003 he won the Fish Prize with his story 'Feathers and Cigarettes'.

Following careers in insurance, computers and full-time motherhood, **Frances McCallum** now divides her time between teaching languages and writing. She works variously and haphazardly on short stories, novels and screenplays, and couldn't bear to give any of them up. She is married with two terrific children and two terrifically boisterous dogs.

Born in Jarrow in 1970, **Justine Mann** now lives in South East London and works as a librarian. She began writing short stories in 2003 and is currently writing a novel.

Leslie Mapp trained as a painter and then spent many years making knight's moves around the education system, teaching, researching, developing, creating. Riding the wave of millennium optimism, he began to concentrate full-time on writing. He lives in North London.

Katherine May is twenty-eight and lives in Rochester, Kent. She took up writing in 2002, and since then has had her stories and poems widely published. In 2005, she won the Folkestone Literary Festival short story prize, and was listed as a winner of the Killie Prize. Her first collection of short stories, *Ghosts and their Uses*, was published in January 2006. She currently works as a creative writing tutor on Tate Britain's schools programme.

Dom Nemer once ate a radish and it gave him heartburn. Today he no longer eats radishes. Instead he writes short stories and occasionally travels the world talking rubbish to anyone who will listen. The rest of the time he's in London eating Jaffa Cakes. Check out his blog: keeponramblin.blogspot.com.

Nick Parker's short stories have been broadcast on BBC Radio 4, and been published in *The Enthusiast, Ambit,* and on www.mcsweeneys.net. More of his work can be found on his website at www.spigmite.net. He is the author of the cult book *Toast: Homage to a Superfood.* In his spare time he is Deputy Editor of *The Oldie* magazine.

Farah Reza works at the City Lit and is training to be an adult education tutor in literature. She is currently working on a novel with the help of the Royal Literary Fund's Writers' Pool and a wonderful writing class run by the Centerprise Literature Development project.

Nina Robertson lives in London and Norfolk. She is studying for an MA in creative writing and is working on a novel set in Puritan New England.

Ray Robinson was born in North Yorkshire in 1971. Ray completed his MA in creative writing at Lancaster with distinction in 1999. He's had poems and short stories published throughout Europe and the Americas and is currently studying for his Ph.D. in creative writing at Lancaster University. An award-winning short-story writer, *Electricity* is his first novel. He lives in London.

Nicholas Royle was born in Manchester in 1963. He is the author of five novels – *Counterparts, Saxophone Dreams, The Matter of the Heart, The Director's Cut* and *Antwerp* – in addition to more than 100 short stories, which have appeared in a wide variety of anthologies and magazines. He has edited twelve anthologies: *Darklands, Darklands 2, A Book of Two Halves, The Tiger Garden: A Book of Writers' Dreams, The Time Out Book of New York Short Stories, The Agony and the Ecstasy: New Writing for the World Cup, The Ex Files: New Stories About Old Flames, Neonlit: Time Out Book of New Writing,*

The Time Out Book of Paris Short Stories, Neonlit: Time Out Book of New Writing Volume 2, The Time Out Book of London Short Stories Volume 2 and *Dreams Never End*. He has written about books, film, art and music for a wide range of publications and is a regular contributor to *Time Out*, the *Independent*, the *Guardian* and the *Independent on Sunday*. He has won the British Fantasy Award three times and the Bad Sex Prize once. He lives in Manchester with his wife and two children. Forthcoming in October 2006 is his first short story collection, *Mortality* (Serpent's Tail). More at www.nicholasroyle.com.

Ella Saltmarshe is an anthropologist by training. Originally from the West Country, she has lived and worked in Spain, Peru and India. She writes, is a film-maker, and works as a freelance communications consultant on social and environmental issues.

Rob Sears, a freelance writer, lives and works in a live/work space in North London. His fiction writing is not substantially published elsewhere.

Pushcart-nominated **Kay Sexton** is an Associate Editor for *Night Train Journal*. Her website www.charybdis.freeserve.co.uk gives details of her current and forthcoming publications, and she has a regular column at www.moondance.org. Her current focus is *Green Thought in an Urban Shade* a collaboration with the painter Fion Gunn to explore and celebrate the parks and urban spaces of Beijing, Dublin, London and Paris in words and images. 'Green Thought' already has exhibitions scheduled in Dublin, London and Paris.

Justine Shaw's Great Grandpa Billy was, until his ninetieth year, a successful travelling sock salesman. Justine, still very much in his shadow, works for an IT company in Kentish Town, likes to swim, and feels far taller than her 5ft $1^{1}/_{2}$ inches.

Ali Smith was born in Inverness in 1962 and lives in Cambridge. She is the author of three collections of stories and three novels, the most recent of which are *The Whole Story and other stories* (Penguin 2004) and *The Accidental* (Penguin 2006).

Margot Stedman was born and raised in Perth, Western Australia, and has worked as lawyer in Sydney, Perth and London, where she has lived for fifteen years. She writes short stories and poetry, and usually finds time to return to Australia every year.

Nick Tucker was born in 1970 and is currently working on a novel, *Albert's Frozen Head*, an extract of which appeared in *Ambit* last year. Nick feels he's never really been given enough credit for inventing electricty, but we've told him this isn't the time or place to get into all that.

Guy Ware has given up on many things – sweeping roads, cleaning toilets, academia, social work, organised Communism, accountancy, photography, playing the trumpet and serving the Crown among them. Fuelled, however, by residual stubbornness, reducing options and a creative writing course at Goldsmiths College, he has completed a stew of stories – under the collective banner *Life's Work* – about murder, fraud, incarceration, blackmail, boredom, politics, filing, disease, insomnia, death and the myriad ways in which work warps our lives and families. 'Cities from a train' is the first part of a trilogy about fathers, sons and butchery. His first novel, *Sitting on top of the world*, will be ready when it's good and ready.

Acknowledgements

Ali Smith's 'The Present' was first published in *The Times* on 24th December 2005.

Nick Parker's 'Field of Ladders' was first published in *Ambit*, Issue 174, 2004.

Sally Foote's 'No Dancing Allowed' was first published in *Time Out London Magazine*, Issue No: 185, 8-15th February 2006.

Patricia Debney's 'After Last Night's Rain' originally appeared in her collection *How to be a Dragonfly* (2005) published by Smith/Doorstep Books.